"Maybe." She spoke with a wistful expression on her face. "Or maybe it was an angel."

"Christmas is a time for miracles, but I haven't had much experience with angels, except the snow kind," Bill said. "I'll stick with magic."

"You do that." She glanced at Liam. "I'm going to stick with my angel the next time I need a Christmas miracle."

Bill wouldn't mind sticking with *her*.

Whoa! Where had that come from?

He wasn't up for sticking with anyone. Not for more than a night. Maybe two if they had fun together.

Maybe the temperature had dropped more than he'd realized. Time to head inside and warm up. He was thinking nonsense right now. "The snow's picking up. Let's warm up inside and make ourselves some hot cocoa. We can check if there's an update on your truck."

Her soft smile kicked his gut with the force of an ornery mountain goat. He forced himself to breathe.

Something was at work here. Not magic. Physical chemistry.

That would explain the way he felt. But he couldn't fool around with Grace—no matter how appealing the thought might be.

Dear Reader,

When I decided to write more stories about a group of volunteer mountain rescuers on Mount Hood, I kept the order of heroes/heroines in my head. After Jake Porter in the first book, I'd write Sean Hughes, Leanne Thomas and then Bill Paulson. After writing Sean's story I was kicking myself that I'd married off Tim Moreno before Jake's book began. In Leanne's story, *Firefighter Under the Mistletoe,* I added a new character—Dr. Cullen Gray—so I could write another story, because I wasn't quite ready to leave Hood Hamlet.

I'm ready now. The time has come to say goodbye to the brave men and women of OMSAR and the quaint Alpine-inspired town of Hood Hamlet, Oregon.

I always knew Bill Paulson's story would be the last book in the series. Bill has been one of my favorite characters, always up for a good time or a laugh, often at his own expense. This Christmas the confirmed bachelor finds more than he bargained for after he helps a young widow named Grace and her three-year-old son, Liam. But with a little Christmas magic—something Hood Hamlet is known for—you never know what might happen!

I want to thank all the readers who fell in love with Hood Hamlet and its inhabitants the way I did. Being asked whose story I was writing next gave me such a great feeling. I must admit typing *The End* in this last book was a bittersweet moment. Although each book in the series stands alone, I've tried to give updates on some of the previous couples and characters.

I hope you enjoy your visit to Hood Hamlet!

Melissa

A Little Bit of Holiday Magic

Melissa McClone

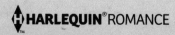

HARLEQUIN® ROMANCE

Recycling programs
for this product may
not exist in your area.

ISBN-13: 978-0-373-74265-3

A LITTLE BIT OF HOLIDAY MAGIC

First North American Publication 2013

Copyright © 2013 by Melissa Martinez McClone

Printed in U.S.A.

With a degree in mechanical engineering from Stanford University, the last thing **Melissa McClone** ever thought she would be doing was writing romance novels. But analyzing engines for a major US airline just couldn't compete with her happily-ever-afters. When she isn't writing, caring for her three young children or doing laundry, Melissa loves to curl up on the couch with a cup of tea, her cats and a good book. She enjoys watching home decorating shows to get ideas for her house—a 1939 cottage that is *slowly* being renovated. Melissa lives in Lake Oswego, Oregon, with her own real-life-hero husband, two daughters, a son, two lovable but oh-so-spoiled indoor cats and a no-longer-stray outdoor kitty that has decided to call the garage home.

Melissa loves to her from her readers. You can write to her at P.O. Box 63, Lake Oswego, OR 97034, USA, or contact her via her website: www.melissamcclone.com.

Recent books by Melissa McClone

THE MAN BEHIND THE PINSTRIPES
WINNING BACK HIS WIFE
HIS LARKVILLE CINDERELLA*
IT STARTED WITH A CRUSH...
FIREFIGHTER UNDER THE MISTLETOE
NOT-SO-PERFECT PRINCESS
EXPECTING ROYAL TWINS!

*Part of *The Larkville Legacy* series

Other titles by this author available in ebook format at www.Harlequin.com.

In Memory of Elizabeth Brooks.
Thank you for the wonderful memories and
always believing I could be a writer.

Special thanks to: Karyn Barr, Roger Carstens,
Alice Burton, Lori Freeland, Lisa Hayden,
Terri Reed, Jennifer Shirk, Margie Lawson and
her Nov. '12 Fab 30 class.

CHAPTER ONE

PLEASE, TRUCK. DON'T die on me.

Grace Bad-luck-is-my-middle-name Wilcox gripped the pickup's steering wheel tighter, as if willpower alone would keep the sputtering engine running in the middle of a blizzard on Mount Hood. A CD of cheery Christmas carols played, but frazzled nerves kept her from singing along.

The tire chains crunched on the snow. The wipers' frenetic back-and-forth struggled to keep the windshield clear of falling snow. The engine coughed, a croupy-seal-bark sound.

She raised her foot off the accelerator.

A gut-clenching grinding noise shook the cab, confirming her fear.

Forget reaching the Oregon coast tonight. The truck wasn't going to survive the drive over Mount Hood.

Stranded in a snowstorm with her three-year-old son.

Shivers racked her body, a mix of panic, fear and bone-chilling cold. The heater had stopped working an hour ago. Her fleece jacket and knit gloves weren't enough to keep her warm.

Grace pressed on the gas pedal, praying for a miracle. She glanced in the rearview mirror to the backseat of the truck's extended cab.

Liam slept in his car seat with his head on a blue stuffed elephant named Peanut, and his body covered with sleeping bags and blankets.

A ball of warmth settled at the center of Grace's chest. Liam—the one bright light in her otherwise dark life. The reason she kept going. "I hope you're having sweet dreams, baby."

Because reality sucked.

Except when you were a little kid and trusted your mom to keep you safe.

And she would keep him safe. That was her job. Though she was failing at being a good mommy tonight.

Liam must be exhausted. It was nearly eleven o'clock, hours past his bedtime, and they'd spent another long day on the road, their progress hampered by harsh winter weather.

"Looks like Astoria will have to wait one more day."

Her voice trembled from the cold, disappointment, fear.

If only we were there now.

The small northern Oregon coastal town, about a three-hour drive from Mount Hood, would be their home. She could make a new life for herself, and most especially, Liam.

With only one working headlight, Grace struggled to see the road due to the wind-driven snow.

The engine clanked and rattled and thunked.

She needed to find a place to stay the night before the truck gave out. She glimpsed something, a pole. No, a sign.

Grace made out the words *Hood Hamlet*. An arrow pointed right.

She had no idea what Hood Hamlet was—she assumed not a Shakespeare character in a hoodie—but anything had to be better than being stuck on the side of the road in this freezing weather all night. She flipped on the blinker, even though no one else was crazy enough to be driving in these conditions, and turned right.

Deep snow. A foot more than was on the highway. No tracks.

The truck plowed ahead, slowed by the road conditions and her nerves. The snow muffled the sounds of the tire chains, but the disturbing engine noises increased in frequency and volume.

Not good.

White-knuckled, she clutched the steering wheel as if it were a lifeline.

Hood Hamlet, please don't let me down.

The snow and darkness, pitch-black except for the one headlight, made seeing more than a foot or two ahead impossible.

She leaned forward, squinting, trying to see.

The windshield fogged on the inside. Frost built up on the outside.

A T in the road lay ahead. But no sign to direct her, nothing to let her know she was close to Hood Hamlet.

Right or left?

Grace chose right. That turn seemed easier to negotiate with the road conditions. She eased the steering wheel toward the passenger's side.

The truck skidded, sliding sideward.

Air rushed from her lungs. Her fingers dug into the steering wheel. "No. No. No."

Turn into the slide.

Hadn't Damon told her that when she was learning to drive? Wait. That was for front-wheel drive cars, not his truck.

She turned the steering wheel the other way.

The truck straightened.

Grace glanced back at Liam, who was still sleeping. "Maybe our luck's changing."

The truck slid again.

She tried to correct, but the vehicle spun in the opposite direction. Round and round, like a merry-go-round with afterburners.

Her pulse accelerated into the stratosphere.

The world passed by in slow motion, appearing through the windshield wipers like blurry photographs.

Trees. Snow. More snow.

Round and round.

Grace couldn't tell what was real, what was her imagination. The roar of her heartbeat drowned out the music.

It'll be okay, babe.

Damon. Tears stung her eyes at the memory of his voice. Nothing had been okay since he'd died.

A wall of snow appeared in front of her.

Every muscle in her body tensed. Panic ricocheted

through her. Grace closed her eyes. She screamed, clutched the steering wheel with all her strength. If only she could hold on to Liam…

"Damon, help us."

A prayer. A plea.

The truck jolted with an awful metallic, crumpling sound. Something exploded, hitting her in the face. A horrible smell filled her nostrils. "Oh."

The engine died.

Liam wailed.

Adrenaline surged. Her face stung. She coughed. "Liam."

He screamed louder. The soul-piercing sound stole her breath and her hope.

Hands shaking, she struggled with her seat belt. The air bag had deflated and lay on her lap. She had to get to her son. "Be right there, baby."

He sobbed, alternating between hiccups and cries, each stabbing her aching heart. "P-nut. Where P-nut?"

"I'll find him." Grace unfastened the belt, turned, reached back. Her face burned. It hurt to breathe. She couldn't see anything, but felt around. "Fleece blanket, cookies, jacket. Peanut has to be here."

She hit the switch on the cab lamp above her.

Light flooded the truck. The engine might not work, but thankfully, the battery still did.

Crocodile tears streamed down Liam's cheeks. "P-nut."

Grace glimpsed blue fuzz stuck between the front and back seats. She pulled out the stuffed animal.

Pushed the elephant into Liam's mitten-covered hands. "Here's Peanut."

The tears stopped flowing. He cuddled his favorite toy. "Mine."

"Do you hurt anywhere?"

"No." He kissed the elephant. "I fine. Peanut fine, too."

A lump clogged her throat. The relief was short-lived. If she didn't do something fast, they were going to freeze.

She tucked blankets and sleeping bags around him again in between coughs.

"Mommy needs to check the truck." And get help. She grabbed her cell phone. Dead. Of course it was. She hadn't been able to find her charger since driving through Utah. "Stay here and keep Peanut warm. I'll be right back."

Grace pulled on her handle. The door wouldn't budge. "Come on."

She tried again. Nothing.

She crawled to the passenger seat and tried that handle. On her third attempt the door opened, pushing away a drift.

Thank goodness. She stumbled out of the truck. Her canvas sneakers sank into the soft snow. Her toes curled from the icy cold.

Wind whipped. Freezing air stung her lungs. Fear doubled with every passing second.

Crossing her arms over her chest and tucking her gloved but trembling hands beneath her armpits, she closed the door with her hip. She needed to keep Liam protected from the cold.

The truck was stuck in a seven-feet-tall snowbank. The shell over the back of the pickup looked fine. She couldn't see the damage to the driver's side, but based on the impact sounds she expected it to be crunched.

"Help," Grace yelled, though she doubted anyone was around. She couldn't see anything in the darkness with snow falling. "Can anyone hear me?"

The wind swallowed her voice. A weight pressed down on her.

She couldn't give up.

Her son needed her to be strong.

If Grace hadn't had Liam, she would have given up the night the army rang her doorbell to tell her Damon, her Ranger husband, a man she'd loved since she was fifteen, had been killed in Afghanistan. Damon had saved three soldiers before dying, but the word *hero* could never fill the gaping hole his death left in her and their son's life. A hole still present two and a half years later.

Damon had always said, *"It'll be okay, babe."*

She repeated his words. *"It'll be okay. It'll be okay."*

All she had to do was find shelter. Get Liam out of the cold. Everything else could wait until daylight.

Grace looked around.

Snow and trees.

That was all she could see.

Stupid snow and stupid trees.

Driving across country from Georgia to Oregon two weeks before Christmas had been stupid. Sure, she'd finally graduated college, but she should have stuck it out another few months until the weather improved.

What was I thinking?

Making new Christmas memories, not dwelling on old ones. Ringing in the New Year in a different place, not wondering what might have been. Meeting new people instead of saying goodbye to old friends transferring out of the Rangers or heading downrange on another deployment, not knowing who wouldn't be coming home this time.

Snow coated her jacket and jeans. Her hair, too. Her gloved hands tingled. She shoved them in her pockets.

"I'm sorry." Her teeth chattered. She blinked away tears. "Should have stayed in Georgia."

It'll be okay, babe.

Grace wished she could believe things would be okay. She glanced back at the truck. At the light illuminating cab. At Liam.

No giving up.

The snow helped the burning sensation on her skin. She wasn't coughing. It no longer hurt to breathe. All good things. And this road had to lead somewhere, to people, right?

She forced her tired legs forward to find help, her feet completely covered in snow. Wetness seeped into her shoes, sending icy chills up her legs.

Grace glanced back at the truck, not wanting to lose sight of her son. Looking forward again, she shielded her eyes from the snowflakes coming at her sideways like miniature daggers. She scanned right to left.

Snow, trees and…

Santa Claus?

She blinked. Refocused.

A lit-up Santa beckoned in the distance. Beyond the figure was a house strung with multicolored Christmas lights.

It'll be okay, babe.

It was going to be okay. At least for tonight. Grace looked up into the swirling snow. "Thank you, Damon."

"No worries. I have power, Mom." Bill Paulson walked out of the kitchen holding a bottle of beer in one hand and the phone against his ear in the other. "This is your third call tonight. It's late. Go to bed. I'll be by in the morning to plow your driveway. I have to check the rental properties, too."

"Unless the snow keeps falling."

Her hopeful words were not unexpected. His mom preferred him stuck inside and safe, rather than on another outdoor adventure. She seemed to forget he was thirty-three, not thirteen. Though, admittedly, sometimes he acted more like a kid than an adult.

"It better stop snowing." He sat in his favorite chair, a big, comfortable leather recliner. Sports highlights played on the TV, with the volume muted. Flames danced and wood crackled in the fireplace. "I don't want to lose another day on the mountain."

A drawn-out, oh-so-familiar sigh came across the line, annoying him like a tickle in the throat before a full-blown cold erupted. He loved his mom, but he knew what was coming next.

"There's more to life than climbing and skiing," she said.

"You don't climb or ski."

"No, but you do."

"My life rocks," Bill said. "There's nothing like helping people in trouble get down the mountain, or carving the first tracks in two feet of fresh powder, then crawling into a comfy, warm bed after a day on the hill."

Especially if he wasn't alone. Which, unfortunately, he was tonight.

"You're headstrong like your father. Always off doing your own thing."

Bill knew that disapproving-mother tone all too well. He'd grown up hearing how much he was like his dad, a man who was never around to support and love her. But this was different. His mom didn't understand the pull of the mountain. The allure of the adrenaline rush. The satisfaction of a successful mission. She was too worried Bill would end up hurt or dead. That could happen one of these days, but still…

Time to change the subject before she laid on another guilt trip. He didn't want to end up letting her down again. "This morning I put up the Santa you brought over. Got the lights strung on the eaves, too."

"Wonderful. How's the tree coming along?"

Two ornaments—a snowboard and a snowshoe— hung from the branches of a seven-foot noble fir. Bill had a box full of more ornaments, but he'd gotten bored trimming the tree. Decorating with a sexy snow bunny for a helper would have been more fun. "The tree's coming along. I've even got a present under there."

He wasn't about to tell his mom the gift was a wedding present for Leanne Thomas and Christian Welton, two firefighters getting married on Saturday. Soon Bill would be the only member of their crew still single.

He didn't mind.

Marriage was fine for other people. Somehow his parents had remained together in spite of spending so much time apart. Maybe when Bill hit forty he would reconsider matrimony as an option. Then again, maybe not. He didn't need another woman dependent on him, like his mom. A woman who would think he wasn't a good enough man, husband, father, and kept waiting for him to screw up.

"I'm happy to finish decorating your tree," Mom said.

He had no doubt she would happily show up to decorate his whole house, wearing an embroidered Christmas sweater and jingle bells dangling from her earlobes. With her husband away most of the time, she focused her attention and energy on Bill. Always had. After she'd miscarried during a difficult pregnancy, she'd turned into a hovering, don't-let-the-kid-out-of-your sight, overprotective mom. His turning eighteen, twenty-one, thirty hadn't lessened the mother hen tendencies. "Give me another week."

"We'll talk tomorrow." She made a smacking sound, her version of a good-night kiss over the phone. "Sleep well, dear."

"Will do." Too bad he'd be sleeping alone. Stormy

nights were perfect for going to bed with a hot woman. But the December dating deadline—the second Monday in December, when men stopped seeing women, in order to avoid spending the holidays with them—had passed. Even friends with benefits expected more than he was willing to give this time of year. "'Night, Mom."

He placed the phone on the end table, sat in the recliner and took a long pull of beer. This year's seasonal brew from the Wy'East Brewing Company went down smoothly.

He glanced at a photograph hanging on the wall—of Jake Porter, Leanne, Nick Bishop, Tim Moreno and himself at Smith Rock during a sunny day of rock climbing in central Oregon. He raised his bottle in memory of Nick, who'd died during a climb on Mount Hood's Reid Headwall at Christmastime nine years ago.

Wind rattled the windows.

Storm, storm, go away. Billy Paulson wants to play.

He downed the rest of the beer.

Game highlights gave way to a sports talk show.

He flipped through the channels, not bothering to turn up the sound. News. Chick flick. Syndicated comedy. The same boring shows.

Bill heard what sounded like a knock.

No one would be out tonight. Must be a branch against the house.

Another knock.

He stood.

The knocking continued. Rapid. Loud.

Not a branch. More like someone in trouble.

Bill ran, opened the door.

Cold wind slammed into his body. Bits of ice pelted his face. Swirling snow blinded his eyes.

He blinked. Focused.

A woman stood on the porch. A woman holding a bunch of blankets. A woman covered with snow.

Bill ushered her inside, then closed the door.

Dark, wet hair obscured her face. Her teeth chattered. Her jeans and jacket were soaked. She wore wet gloves.

He brushed snow off her jacket, icy wetness chilled his palms. "What's going on?"

"S-slid into a s-snowbank."

"Were you buckled up?"

"Yes."

"Did you hit your head?"

"No. Air b-bag."

"Back or neck pain?"

"No."

"Does anything hurt?"

"F-f-face was b-burning. H-hard to breathe. B-but that's better now." She shivered. "Just c-c-old."

Bill pushed the wet hair off her face to get a better look at her.

Wide amber eyes. Flushed cheeks. Runny nose.

Full, generous lips.

The kind of lips a man, at least this man, dreamed about tasting and kissing and…

Her lips trembled.

Focus, Paulson. "Let's get you out of that wet jacket."

She held out the pile of blankets. "M-m-my s-son."

Adrenaline shot through Bill. He grabbed the child and laid him on the rug in front of the living room fireplace. "Is he injured?"

"I d-don't think so."

Bill peeled away the wet top covering. "How old is he?"

She struggled out of her gloves and pink fleece jacket, nothing more than a waterlogged sponge now. "Three."

Another blanket came off, this one dryer than the last. "What's his name?"

The woman slipped off canvas sneakers. She wasn't wearing socks. Not exactly dressed for the weather. What in the world was she doing driving around in a snowstorm?

"Liam." She stepped away from the puddle of water pooling by her shoes. "I'm G-Grace. Grace Wilcox."

"Bill Paulson."

"Mommy," a small, scared voice said from beneath a blue fleece blanket.

Grace kneeled next to the boy. She wore a short-sleeved T-shirt. Goose bumps covered her arms. "R-right here, honey."

Bill raised the blue blanket. "Liam?"

A small boy with dark hair and pale skin looked up with quarter-size blue eyes. He wore red mittens and forest-green footie pajamas.

Bill gave the kid his best fireman smile. "Hello, little dude."

Liam's lips quivered. "Mommy."

Grace pulled his mitten-covered hand onto her lap. "It's okay."

Okay? Only if she was talking about them being out of the storm. Maybe she had hit her head or maybe she was drunk.

Bill didn't smell alcohol. She didn't show any obvious signs of impairment, except for driving late at night in a blizzard. "Was Liam in a car seat?"

Her do-I-look-like-a-bad-mother glare hit Bill like an ice pick in the forehead. "Of course my son was in a car seat. He was in the backseat."

"Just a question." Bill didn't see any cuts or bruises. "No offense intended."

He touched the boy's shoulder.

She grabbed the top of Bill's hand, her fingers, as cold as Popsicles, dug into his skin. "What are you doing?"

"Checking your son." Bill didn't need to look over to know an anxious mother was watching his every move. "I'm a firefighter with Hood Hamlet Fire and Rescue. I have EMT training and am a wilderness first responder with OMSAR."

"OMSAR?"

Definitely not from around here if she didn't know what that was. He shot her a sideways glance. Anxious, but attractive with wide-set eyes, high cheekbones, straight nose and full lips. Mid-twenties, if that. "Oregon Mountain Search and Rescue."

Her gaze went from distrustful to relieved. "Looks like I picked the right house."

"Da-arn straight." Bill didn't want to curse in front

of the kid. "No visible signs of trauma. Does anything hurt, buddy?"

The little guy scrunched up his nose. "P-Nut."

Bill looked at Grace. "Huh?"

"Peanut is right here." She handed the child a stuffed animal. "Tell Mr. Paulson if anything hurts, okay?"

The kid's eyes glistened. Tears would fall in 3…2…1.

"Tummy." Liam's voice cracked.

Internal injury? Bill's throat tightened. "I need to check Liam's abdomen."

Color drained from the woman's face. She rubbed her hands over her mouth. "Maybe we should call 9-1-1."

"I am 9-1-1, minus the truck, flashing lights and uniform." Bill grabbed the pajama zipper and pulled. "Relax. I know what I'm doing. If he needs help, we'll get it."

"Hungry," Liam said.

Bill's hand stalled. "You want something to eat?"

The little boy nodded.

"Wanting food is a good sign." Bill examined Liam. No redness or marks from where the car seat straps may have hit his body. No signs of distress or shock or concussion. The kid seemed fine. "How does a cookie sound?"

A grin brighter than the lights on the Christmas tree erupted on the kid's face. "Cookie! I want cookie, puh-lease."

Bill's throat relaxed, allowing him to breathe easier. The kid was going to be okay. But the mom was another story. Not quite panicked, but cold and suspicious.

The dark circles under her eyes told only half the story. Exhausted, check. Stressed, check. Nervous, two checks. Her eyes darted back and forth, unable to focus on one thing too long. But with each pass, her gaze lingered on him a second longer than the last. Her wariness pissed him off. She seemed to forget *she'd* knocked on *his* door tonight.

"Do you want a cookie?" he asked. "Chocolate chip. My mom made them."

Grace gnawed on her lip. "No, thanks."

Bill rose. He grabbed two chocolate chip cookies from the snowman-shaped cookie jar on the kitchen counter, then returned to the living room. He handed one to Liam, who'd removed his mittens, and the other to Grace, who looked as if he'd given her a grenade with the pin pulled.

Her confused gaze bounced from the cookie to Bill. "I didn't want one."

"You look like you need one." He watched Liam munch his cookie. "Nothing wrong with his appetite."

"Unless I'm trying to feed him veggies."

Grace's lighthearted tone surprised Bill, but it was good to see her sense of humor come out. "Who wants to eat icky green and orange things?" he asked.

The kid and Peanut nodded.

"Green and orange *things*—" Grace emphasized the last word "—help a person grow to be tall and strong. I'm sure Mr. Paulson didn't become a firefighter by eating junk food and drinking soda."

Grace sounded like a mom. Duh. She was one. He wasn't helping her out here. "Your mom's correct, Liam. Eat lots of vegetables, fruit and protein if you want to grow up to be tall and strong like me."

She stared down her nose at Bill. "Modest."

Her tone and look screamed *not interested*. That only piqued his. "Humility is a virtue."

Grace opened her mouth, but didn't say a word. She looked away, then took a bite of her cookie.

Bill knelt next to her. Wet hair dampened Grace's shirt. She wasn't busty, but had curves in the places that mattered. She smelled good in spite of being wet, a mix of vanilla and cinnamon and something he couldn't place. "Let's see how you're doing."

Holding the cookie, she crossed her arms tight over her chest. "I'm okay. The snow washed away the powder from the air bag."

"Looking you over won't take long."

She scooted back. "I'm good."

He cut the distance between them. "Let me make sure."

Grace stood. Every motion seemed to take effort. A battle of fatigue and stress and shock, one she was losing. "You've done enough."

His gaze ran the length of her, checking for obvious injuries. He didn't see any. "Show me where the seat belt straps hit you."

"It's not necessary. I told you, the air bag—"

"If you stiffened prior to impact, you're going to be sore."

"I'm—"

"I'm trying to do my job here. That's all. Please let me examine you." He was losing patience. "I have to determine if you need to go to the hospital tonight."

She nibbled on her lip.

"Would it make a difference if I put on my uniform?" he asked.

"None whatsoever." Her firm voice left no doubt she was serious. "I appreciate you letting us get warm, but I need to find a place to stay tonight."

"You're not going anywhere unless it's the hospital."

She glanced out the window. "But—"

"The weather's wicked. You're staying here tonight. I'll keep an eye on you."

Forget deer in headlights. Grace's expression made her look as if she'd been flattened by a semi. "That's—"

"Your only option."

Her mouth twisted.

He wasn't deterred. "I have two spare bedrooms. Use one or both." Bill pointed to her coat. "You may feel warmer without your wet jacket and shoes, but you need to change clothes."

Grace rubbed the back of her neck.

"Sore?" he asked.

"Fine." She moistened her lips. "All my clothes are in the truck."

"I have something you can wear. Be right back." Bill sprinted to his bedroom and grabbed a pair of flannel pajamas, a Christmas gift last year from his parents. Well, from his mom. His dad usually arrived home on Christmas Eve and was out the door on the twenty-sixth, leaving Bill to become his mom's entire world again. Maybe if he'd had a sibling, a little brother or sister, things would be different. Better. But Bill hadn't called for help soon enough. His mother had lost her baby and couldn't have another.

Back in the living room, he handed the pajamas to Grace. "They'll be big on you."

She stared at them as if he'd handed her a French maid outfit to wear, complete with fishnet stockings and a feather duster.

Her jaw tightened. "You want me to wear your pajamas?"

He pressed his lips together to keep from smiling. "They're practically new. I've only worn the bottoms a couple times. Flannel is warm. You might be hypothermic."

Her suspicious gaze targeted him once more. It was a good thing she wasn't armed, or he would be a goner.

"You're really a firefighter and mountain rescuer?"

"Check the pictures on the mantel." He pointed to framed articles and photographs. "And the walls."

Looking around, Grace held the pajamas in front of her like a shield.

Okay, he got it. Got her.

No wedding ring, and a kid had made her cautious. That was smart. She didn't know him. Didn't know her having a child meant he considered her off-limits, a look-don't-touch, modern-day leper.

"My job is to help people in trouble. I do that when I'm on the mountain, too," he said. "That's all I'm trying to do here."

"It's just…" Grace glanced at Liam, who was playing with Peanut. She touched the boy's head. "I've never been stranded—with a stranger."

"No worries. I understand. But you're safe here. If it makes you feel any better, the bedroom doors lock."

Her eyes darkened. "From the inside or outside?"

That would be funny if she didn't sound so serious. "I have an idea. I'll call the sheriff's office. Let them know about your truck, so they can get it towed. Then you can talk to the sheriff or a deputy. They'll appease your concerns about staying here tonight."

"The sheriff and his deputies will vouch for you?" Only a deaf person would miss her please-someone-tell-me-he's-not-psychotic plea.

"I've lived in Hood Hamlet my whole life. I know everybody."

Grace's gaze took in the articles and photographs hanging on the wall again. The tension in her face, especially around her mouth, lessened. "Okay. Let's call the sheriff. I doubt there's more than one black pickup stuck in a snowbank around here, but in case there is, mine has Georgia plates."

"Long way from home."

She shrugged.

Must be a story there. Not his business.

Even if he was curious…

CHAPTER TWO

FIVE MINUTES LATER, Bill took the phone from Grace, who held on to his pajamas with her other hand. The lines creasing her forehead had disappeared, but the wariness in her eyes remained. He hoped that look wasn't due to something the sheriff had said. "All good now?"

"The sheriff said Liam and I would be safe with you." Her voice sounded stronger, but her words had a nervous edge. She rubbed her fingertips against the pajamas. "He's going to take care of my truck."

"Truck," Liam repeated. "I like trucks. Big ones."

"Me, too." The kid was cute. So was the mom. If she would quit acting as if Bill was a murderer. She shifted her weight from foot to foot. At least her toes weren't frostbitten. "Something's still bothering you."

Her hands stopped fidgeting with the pajamas. "You're perceptive."

"Sometimes." Bill wasn't about to play games with Grace after what she'd been through. "Tell me what's going on."

She looked at Liam, looked at his EMT and wilderness first aid books on the shelf, a snowboard, an old fire helmet, looked at everything in the living room except Bill.

He took a step closer. "Something's got you wigged out."

Grace rubbed her lips together. "The sheriff thinks you should, um, check me. See if we…I…need to go to the hospital."

That would do it. "Good idea."

"No. I don't. Need to go, that is." Her gaze still avoided his. "I'm a little sore. Nothing else."

Liam played with Peanut, seemingly oblivious to everything else.

"Most people are sore after an accident." Bill didn't know if she was afraid of going to the hospital or of him. He'd guess the latter, but wished she'd look at him so he could try to see if something else was going on with her. "The rush of adrenaline can mask injuries. You should be examined."

Grace nodded, but looked as if she'd rather face a dentist and gynecologist at the same time than be checked by him. She ran her teeth over her lower lip.

"I promise I don't bite," he teased.

She blushed. Her bright red cheeks made her look like a teenager.

He motioned to a chair. "Do you want to sit?"

"I'd rather stand."

Figures. When Bill was on a call or out in the field on a rescue mission, he tried to keep the patient at ease. Joking around with Grace wasn't working. He'd try talking to her. "Where do you live in Georgia?"

"Columbus."

"You don't sound Southern."

"I grew up in the Midwest. Iowa."

"Cornfields and the Iowa Hawkeyes."

Her amber eyes twinkled. "And country fairs."

"Let me guess. You were the Corn Queen."

Her grin brightened her face. Not only pretty, unexpectedly beautiful.

Air stuck in his throat. He struggled to breathe.

She struck a royal pose, lifting her chin and shifting her shoulders back. "Corn Princess."

Bill had no idea why he'd reacted to her. Must be tired. "Sash and tiara?"

"Corn-on-the-cob scepter, too."

"Real Iowan corn?"

"Only the finest." She gave Liam a royal wave. "I was the envy of the corn court until an unfortunate incident with one of the 4-H goats."

"Poor goat."

"Poor corn." She made an exaggerated sad face. "After the goat encounter, I was a princess without a scepter."

Okay, this was more like it. Smiling and joking and raising Bill's temperature ten degrees. "So what brings her highness out of the land of sweet tea and juicy peaches across the Mississippi River and over the Rockies to the verdant Pacific Northwest?"

She stared at Liam. Her eyes softened. "Astoria."

"Ah. Nice little coastal town, if you don't mind being at sea level." Bill preferred living in the mountains. "Do you have family there?"

"No, but I thought why not try something different." Her voice sounded shaky. Nerves?

Or something more? "That's a big move."

She shrugged, but tight lines formed around her mouth. "I've moved a lot."

"I've moved twice, not counting my stint at the fire academy. Once from my parents' house to an apartment, then into this house." Bill stood next to Grace. The top of her head came to the tip of his nose. "Show me where you're sore."

She pointed to her left shoulder, where the seat belt would have hit.

He touched the spot. "Does this hurt?"

"Slightly tender." She glanced at his hand on her, then looked away. "I can't remember all the moves we've made. My husband was in the army."

Was. Past tense. She hadn't said ex-husband, but she wasn't wearing a wedding band. Bill knew some folks didn't wear rings. Others lost them. Or pawned them. "Is your husband waiting for you in Astoria?"

She bent down and stroked Liam's hair. "He's... dead."

Her words cut Bill at the knees. He opened his mouth to apologize, to say something, anything, but nothing came out. She was so young with a kid.

Just like Hannah, Nick's wife.

A million memories rushed back, memories Bill had hoped to forget. The smell of death when his rescue team had found the bodies of Nick and Iain, still roped together. The sound of grief when he'd spent days at Nick's house, trying to comfort the Bishop family. The taste of regret when Bill had realized nothing he did or said would make things better for Hannah and her two young kids.

He had felt so useless back then. He forced himself to breathe now. At least he could do something for Grace. "I'm sorry."

"Thank you." The words came automatically, as if programmed in and spoken without thinking.

Her gaze, full of affection, remained on Liam, who kept himself entertained with the toy elephant.

Bill thought he could reach out and touch the love she was sending her son. A small knot formed in his chest. Ached behind his ribs. He didn't know what was going on, but he didn't like how he wanted to hold Grace until she looked at him the same way.

Not that she would. He had a habit of failing the women in his life. Just like his dad.

"Columbus, Georgia." Bill forced the words from his dry throat. "Is that where your husband was stationed?"

"Yes. Fort Benning. Damon was a Ranger. He was killed in action in Afghanistan two and a half years ago."

Damn. That sucked. "A real hero."

"Yes. Highly decorated. He loved what he did."

Grace's affection for her late husband filled her voice. Love never played into Bill's relationships. He much preferred the other *L* word. *Lust*. Love was too messy, too complicated. It was capable of causing pain and grief, like Grace must have endured with her husband's death. "Our service members have paid a high price in the Middle East, but your husband leaves behind a legacy of memories, and Liam."

Her gaze went from her son to Bill. "Is there, um, anything else you need to check?"

He looked at his hand on her shoulder. Damn. Still touching her. He lowered his arm. "Any headache or sore neck now?"

"No."

If her headrest wasn't set properly she could have whiplash. He rubbed his hands together so they wouldn't be cold against her skin, and stepped behind her. "I'm going to move your hair to check your neck."

"That's fine." Her tight tone made him think otherwise.

Bill pushed her long wet hair over to one side. His fingertips brushed her neck.

She inhaled sharply. Tensed.

"Sorry." He liked the feel of her soft skin. If only she wasn't so cold. But he knew ways to warm her up. Lots of ways.

Stop. Right there.

Bill might have the reputation of being a player, but he didn't play with patients. He touched her neck again. "Does this area hurt?"

Her back stiffened. "Not really."

He wasn't buying it. "You feel something."

"Nothing major." She sounded nonchalant, as if she had a splinter in her finger, nothing more. "A dull ache."

He moved his hand lower. "What about here?"

"Very dull. Almost nothing."

He moved in front of her. "Show me where the seat belt hit you."

Grace pointed to her left shoulder, then diagonally across her chest and over her hips.

"Does your abdomen or lower back hurt?"

"No."

"Hips?"

"All good."

"We can hold off a trip to the hospital tonight. Depending on how you feel tomorrow, you might want to see a doctor."

"Okay."

"Time for you to get out of those wet clothes. You can change in the bathroom. First door on the right." Bill motioned to Liam. "The little dude and I will make cocoa."

Liam clapped the elephant's paws together. "Cocoa. Cocoa."

Bill offered her the phone. "Take this with you. You can call whoever you need to, and let them know what's happened."

Sadness filled her gaze. "Thanks, but there's no one to call."

With that, Grace walked down the hall. Denim clung to her hips, showing off her curves and the sway of her hips.

Nice butt.

Hot.

Whoa.

Not going to happen. Not with a mom. Definitely not with a widow.

He liked rescuing damsels in distress, but only long enough to see them back on their feet and be rewarded for his efforts. He might help moms, but he didn't date them. Ever.

Mothers with children equaled commitment.

He'd rather hang in base camp, drinking and playing cards, than attempt that summit. Married friends might be happy, but they had provided enough *beta* on the climb. Marriage took commitment and hard work. An instant family wasn't on Bill's list of peaks to bag.

Hot or not, Grace and her son were his houseguests, period.

The bathroom door closed.

Liam sidled up next to Bill, pressing against his leg. He glanced down. "Guess it's you and me, kid."

Liam held up his elephant.

"And Peanut." The expectant look in the little boy's eyes reminded Bill of the schoolkids who toured the station on field trips. Sitting behind the steering wheel wasn't enough. Sirens needed to blare and lights flash. And helmets. The kids all had to wear the helmet. "I bet you want another cookie."

"Please. Cocoa, too."

Kids were the same whether they came from Hood Hamlet, Oregon, or Columbus, Georgia. "Marshmallows or whipped cream?"

"Both."

A small hand clasped Bill's larger one. Squeezed.

Warmth shot up his arm. Boy, that felt good. And not because Liam's tiny fingers weren't so cold any longer.

Inquisitive eyes full of adoration gazed up at Bill, making him feel like a superhero.

Something tugged inside his chest. Something he'd

never experienced before. Something he didn't understand. He shook off the unfamiliar and unwelcome feeling.

Must be all the excitement around here.

This wasn't the evening he'd expected to spend. A cute kid wanting to make hot chocolate with him in the kitchen. A pretty mom changing into his pajamas in the bathroom. But Bill was not unhappy the way tonight was turning out.

Company and cookies and cocoa beat decorating the Christmas tree any day.

Even at midnight.

It's going to be okay.

In the bathroom, Grace repeated Damon's words. She stripped out of her clothes and dried herself off with a blue towel hanging on the rack.

Why wouldn't it be okay?

She was naked, standing in a strange man's house, about to put on a strange man's pajamas, wondering if the strange man was too good to be true.

According to the sheriff, Bill Paulson was a kind, caring, generous man. She shouldn't be surprised, since she believed Damon had helped her find this refuge from the storm.

But she doubted her late husband would appreciate the hum racing through her body. A hum that had nothing to do with the drive or the crash or the strangeness of the night, and everything to do with her handsome rescuer. The only way to describe the feeling was first-date jitters. Except this was no date. And Bill…

He reminded her of Damon. The two men had similar coloring and take-charge personalities. Bill exuded the same strength, confidence and heat as her husband.

Too bad the similarities ended there.

Damon had always been attractive, but his looks became rugged over the years due to scars from shrapnel and a nose broken twice. Not exactly world-weary, but not happy-go-lucky like Bill Paulson, whose gorgeous features belonged on the pages of an outdoor magazine layout. Bill wasn't quite a pretty boy, especially with the sexy razor stubble, but close.

No doubt she was in shock.

That would explain her noticing every little thing about him. Reacting, too.

Touching Bill's hand had felt good, his skin warm and rough against hers. His touching her had felt even better, his hand on her shoulder, calming and sure, as if it belonged there.

But when he'd touched her neck…intimate, almost sexual, albeit unintentional…

She missed…that. A man's touch.

Don't think about him.

At least not *that* way.

Annoyed with herself, she shrugged on the pajama shirt. The soft flannel brushed her like a caress. The friction of fabric over dry skin warmed her, even though the pajamas were too big.

The sleeves hung over her hands. She rolled them to her wrists, then fastened the front buttons with trembling fingers. Her hands didn't shake from the cold, but from the situation.

Nerves.

She stepped into the pants. The hems pooled at her feet. She cuffed them.

The waistband slid down her hips. She rolled the top, determined to make this work.

Nerves weren't her only issue. A touch of guilt, too. *Something's got you wigged out.*

Yeah, him.

Of all the houses on Mount Hood, she would pick the one belonging to a firefighter and mountain rescuer. The hottest guy she'd been alone with since, well, Damon had deployed.

Grace grimaced at her starstruck reflection. Had she looked this goofy while talking to Bill? She hoped not. Either way, she was being silly, acting like a teenager with a crush, not an adult, not a mom.

So what if Bill Paulson was a nice piece of eye candy? So what if he had a killer smile? So what if the concern in his bright, baby-blue eyes for her and Liam had sent an unexpected burst of heat rushing through her veins?

Tomorrow he would be one more person who had passed through her life. Nothing more.

All she had to do was survive tonight.

How hard could that be?

Grace shuffled from the bathroom and down the hallway, the carpet runner soft beneath her feet.

In the living room, a sense of warmth and homey goodness surrounded her. She'd been so frantic earlier she hadn't noticed the house. Now she took in the hardwood floors, beamed ceiling, river rock fireplace, wood mantel covered with photographs, and beautifully lit Christmas tree.

She wiggled her toes.

More cabin than house.

Inviting and comfortable.

The kind of place she'd dreamed of living someday. The kind of place where a kid could grow up happy. The kind of place a family could call home.

The scent of the Christmas tree hung in the air along with a touch of smoke from the burning fire. The beer bottle on the wooden end table and the gigantic leather recliner seemed typical for a bachelor pad, but the couch with color-contrasting pillows and coordinating throw blanket seemed out of place for a guy living alone. A far cry from her cheap apartment in Columbus.

Was there a girlfriend or wife in the picture? Maybe an ex who had lived here and decorated?

Male laughter, rich and deep and smooth, washed over her like water from a hot shower, heating her from the outside in. Forget feeling warm; she was downright feverish.

She'd forgotten the appeal of a man's laugh, the happiness and humor contagious. A higher pitched squeal joined in. That laugh, one she knew better than her own, brought a smile to her lips.

Liam.

Her chest tightened.

He could be such a serious boy. She was pleased he was having so much fun.

Grace entered the charming kitchen, with its dining area separated by a breakfast bar.

Bill sat at the table with her son, who was wrapped in a blanket, his little hands around a mug. Peanut sat on the table with his own mug in front of him.

What kind of guy would fix a cup of hot chocolate for a stuffed animal?

The sheriff had told her Bill Paulson was a cross between an Eagle Scout and an X Games champ. Yeah, that seemed to sum him up.

Grace moved behind Liam. She placed her hands on his narrow shoulders. "It looks like you boys did fine on your own."

Bill stood, his manners excellent. "Your cocoa is on the counter."

She noticed the steaming mug. "Liam doesn't drink his very hot."

"I've been around kids. I put ice cubes in his and Peanut's cups in case they decided to share."

She appreciated his treating Peanut like a living, breathing elephant, not a stuffed one. "Liam could spill on your blanket."

"It's washable. Isn't that right, little dude?"

Liam looked up at Bill. Her son had a case of hero worship. "That's right, big dude."

"Okay, then." Grace took her cup from the counter and sipped. "This is delicious."

Bill raised his cup. "My mom makes her own cocoa mix."

Liam took another sip. "It's yum."

Interesting. Her son seemed perfectly content to be away from her. Usually he didn't want to be out of eyesight.

A twinge of regret pinched Grace's heart. She'd done everything she could to be a good parent, but that didn't seem to be enough. Liam liked having Bill—a man—around. Well, her son better enjoy the company because tomorrow they would be on their own again.

"You have a very nice home." She wouldn't expect a single guy's house to be so clean, with homemade cocoa and cookies at the ready. "Thanks for everything."

Bill gave her the once-over.

Grace knew better than to be flattered, especially since she couldn't tell what he thought of her. Probably not much, given she was wearing his baggy pajamas, had no makeup on and her hair was a scraggly mess.

Her appearance wasn't due only to traveling. She hadn't cared how she looked since Damon died. She couldn't remember the last time she'd had her hair cut. She hadn't thought about her hair, her nails, her looks.

Until now.

She combed her fingers through damp strands, all too aware of how she'd let herself go these past two and a half years. Not that she wanted a man in their life. She could have stayed in Columbus and married Kyle if she'd wanted a husband.

Liam needs a father. You need a husband. You'll grow to love me.

As if saying "I do" was all it took to make a marriage work. Grace shook the memory of Staff Sergeant Kyle Gabriel's proposal from her mind. She dropped her hand to her side. "I don't know how I'll repay you for tonight."

"No need." Bill motioned to the empty chair next

to Liam. "Send me a postcard once you're settled in Astoria, and we'll call it good."

Relief washed over Grace, grateful that he hadn't asked for more, for something she might not want to give. A postcard would be easy. She would have to remember to get his address. She sat. "I can manage that."

"You mentioned trying something different by moving to Astoria. Why there and not a bigger city?"

"The Goonies."

"Excuse me?"

"There's a movie called *The Goonies*," she explained. "When I was dating my husband, Damon was saving money to buy his truck, so we didn't go out on dates that cost a lot of money. One time he came over to my house to watch movies. We saw *The Goonies.* Damon said when we got married we should go to Astoria for our honeymoon."

"Astoria, Oregon?"

She shrugged, waiting for hot tears to prick her eyes. Surprisingly, they didn't come. Sadness and grief ebbed like the tides. "It sounded cool to a couple of kids from Iowa. We didn't have the money for a honeymoon after we eloped. We got married at city hall. Two excited kids—me in my Sunday best and Damon in his army dress uniform–with a bouquet of carnations and two plain gold wedding bands. Going to Astoria ended up on our to-do list."

"You and your son are doing it now."

Grace nodded. She thought Damon would approve. Liam yawned.

She took the mug from his hand. A preemptive move. "Tired, baby?"

He shook his head. "P-nut tired. He ready for nighty-night."

"It's been a long day for Peanut. You, too." Bill pulled out Liam's chair. "I'll show you the guest rooms."

"One room is fine." She stared at the dirty cups and spoons on the table. "Less of a mess to clean up tomorrow."

"Help yourself to the spare toothbrushes and toothpaste in the bathroom drawer."

"Have a lot of unexpected guests?" she asked.

"Not a lot, but I like to be prepared." He winked. "You never know who might knock on the door."

His tone teased, but Grace doubted his houseguests were stranded like her and Liam. Most likely they were attractive young females eager to spend the night.

The realization unsettled her.

Maybe she was wrong.

For all she knew, he had a girlfriend or a fiancée. The thought didn't make her feel better.

"Thanks. I appreciate your hospitality. I hope having us here won't cause you any problems with your… girlfriend."

"No worries," he said. "I don't have a girlfriend."

Yay. Single. Grace stiffened. Being happy he was available was a crazy reaction, but oh well. She was only human.

And out of his league.

She needed a haircut, a good night's sleep, a job

and the ability to converse with a hot guy without losing her cool.

Not only out of his league, in a different grade. Grace was a kindergartner when dealing with the opposite sex. Bill was working on his master's thesis.

"Come on, Liam." She reached for her son. "Let's get you to bed."

Liam held his arms out to Bill.

Hurt flashed through Grace. Her chest tightened. She struggled to breathe.

"What can I say?" Bill's smile lit up his face and took her breath away. "Kids love me."

"Women, too?" The words came out before Grace could stop them. She wanted to cringe, hide, run away. But where was she going to go? She swallowed a sigh.

Bill's lopsided grin defined the word *charming*. "Most women. Except those who think I'm a psychotic killer."

He meant her. His lighthearted tone told Grace he wasn't upset. If anything, he made her suspicions sound…endearing. But she was still embarrassed.

"I'll carry him to the guest room." He lifted Liam up. "Don't forget Peanut."

Liam hugged the elephant and settled comfortably in Bill's arms, against Bill's chest. "Peanut like to be carried."

"Good," Bill said. "Because I like to carry."

Watching the two was bittersweet for Grace. The last time Damon had carried their son, Liam had been a year old, barely walking. Babbling, not talking.

Don't look back.

Grace was moving west to start over. She couldn't change the past. Damon was never coming back. She needed to look forward for both her and Liam's sake.

She followed Bill down the hallway to a room with a queen-size cherry sleigh bed and matching dresser and nightstand. A patchwork quilt covered the bed, with coordinating shams on the pillows. Framed pictures hung on the wall. The room sure beat a cheap motel with paper-thin walls, or an expensive hotel she couldn't afford.

"This is lovely." But odd considering the house belonged to a single guy. "Did you decorate the room yourself?"

"My mom helped me with the entire house. She thought my apartment was too much a man cave. I give her full credit for making sure everything coordinated."

"Your mother did a good job."

Holding Liam with one arm, Bill pulled down the covers. He gently set the little boy on the bed. "There you go, bud."

Liam thrust out his lower lip. "Not tired. More cocoa and cookies."

"I'll take you to the bathroom," Grace said. "Then I bet you and Peanut will be ready for bed."

At least she hoped so, because she didn't think her heavy eyelids would remain open much longer. Her feet ached for rest. Her brain wanted to shut down for the night.

"Want Bill." Liam's tiny fingers wiggled, reaching for the firefighter. "P-nut want Bill, too."

Grace opened her mouth to speak, but couldn't. This was the first time Liam had asked for someone else. She tried to ignore the prick of hurt, telling herself this was no big deal.

Bill knelt next to the bed, giving her son the height advantage. "Listen. I'm going to be in the room next to the bathroom. That's across the hall. When you wake up, we can have breakfast. Chocolate chip pancakes sound good?"

Liam nodded about a hundred times.

"We'll make a snowman if the storm lets up." Bill stood. "But you and Peanut need to be well rested, okay?"

Another nod from Liam. This time Peanut joined in.

Grace mouthed a thank-you.

Bill stepped away from the bed. "Give me your keys. I'll get your suitcases out of the truck."

She thought for a moment, touched her hand to her face. "Oh, no. I left the keys in the ignition. I wasn't thinking straight."

"You've been through a lot."

He had no idea. "Our suitcase is on the floor in front of the passenger seat. Everything else we own is in the back."

Compassion filled his eyes, not the usual pity people lavished on a widow.

She appreciated that.

Bill glanced toward the window. "Under a tarp or do you have a shell?"

"Shell."

"I hope there aren't any cracks from the accident."

"If there are, I don't want to know." She looked at Liam, who was bouncing Peanut on the bed as if the mattress was a trampoline. "Not until morning."

Bill drew his hand across his mouth as if he were zipping his lips.

The gesture was kidlike and sweet at the same time. "Thanks."

His gaze rested on Liam. "It's not easy being a single parent."

The sincerity of Bill's voice made Grace wonder if he knew someone who'd lost a spouse. She thought about asking, but didn't want to pry. "You do what you have to do. I'm not the first wife to have lost her husband. Or Liam his father."

"It still sucks."

Bill's words cut through the pleasantries—aka crap—people said to her, trying to make the bad stuff bearable. "Yes, it does. But you're right about having memories and Liam. That's made all the difference. And now we have our own Ranger angel looking out for us. Damon definitely had our six tonight."

A thoughtful expression formed on Bill's face. "You're lucky you walked away from that snowbank without any injuries."

"True, but that's not what I meant." Grace smiled up at him, a smile straight from her heart, something usually reserved for Liam alone. "I was talking about us finding you."

CHAPTER THREE

THE SMELL OF freshly brewed coffee enticed Grace to open her heavy eyelids. The scent made her mouth water and her tummy grumble. A cup of java and one of Damon's banana walnut muffins sounded so—

Wait a minute.

Her husband was dead. She was in bed.

Who made the coffee?

She blinked, disoriented and confused.

Light filtered through the window blinds. Not her apartment. Not anyplace she recognized.

Grace bolted upright.

Tall dresser, closet door, closed bedroom door.

Memories of the night before exploded in her mind. Driving in the blizzard. Crashing into the snowbank. Stumbling to Bill Paulson's front door. She hadn't been dreaming. Last night had been real.

Grace stretched her sleep-drenched arms and arched her back, like a drowsy cat waking from a much-needed nap.

She'd slept through the night. No bad dreams to wake her.

Amazing, considering she hadn't had a full night's

sleep since Damon's death, and odd, since she was sleeping in a strange house in a stranger's guest room. Maybe this move to Astoria hadn't been the worst idea since skinny jeans.

Wind shook the window. The storm hadn't let up.

"We sure aren't in Columbus anymore, baby."

Grace moved her hand to the right to touch her son. Her fingers hit the mattress. "Liam?"

The spot next to her was empty.

No Liam.

No Peanut.

Her stomach clenched. Her heartbeat roared in her ears. "Liam."

No answer.

A million and one thoughts raced through her head, none of them good.

She scrambled out of bed, threw open the door and raced down the hallway. Every muscle bunched.

The sheriff had vouched for Bill Paulson. She'd been taken with the handsome firefighter herself. But Bill wasn't used to having kids in the house. What if he'd left cleaning solution where Liam could reach it? What if he'd left a door unlocked and Liam had wandered out of the house? What if? What if? What if?

Every nerve ending twitched. Her stomach roiled. She thought she might be physically ill.

It'll be okay, babe.

If only she could believe that.

"You'd better not do that again, Liam." Bill's voice, loud and boisterous, sounded from the kitchen. "I'm warning you."

Liam wasn't outside, but the knowledge didn't loosen the tension in her shoulders. Something was going on.

Grace accelerated her pace, lengthening her stride. She rounded the corner. Skidded to a stop.

On the floor between the dining area and breakfast bar, Bill sat crisscross applesauce with Liam and at least thirty dominoes set up in a row.

"I mean it this time." Bill tried to sound serious, but his mouth curved upward, a big grin tugging at his lips. "Don't touch the dominoes!"

Defiance gleamed in Liam's gaze. Mischief, too. He raised his arm, made a small fist and pushed over the first domino. The rest cascaded one on top of the other.

"You did it again!" Bill placed his hand over his heart and tumbled to the floor as if he'd been knocked over, too. "What are we going to do, Peanut? Liam won't listen."

Her son giggled.

The sheer delight in his voice warmed Grace's insides. Her pulse slowed. Her heart rate returned to normal. A bolt of guilt flashed through her at being so quick to think the worst of Bill Paulson when she'd woken up without Liam next to her.

Liam clapped. "Again. Again."

"Okay, kid. But only for you." Bill reset the dominoes, a job that took patience and a steady hand. "One more time."

Liam spread his fingers. "Ten more."

Grace wondered how many times they'd played this game. Knowing Liam, at least ten, but Bill didn't seem to mind.

"Two more," Bill countered. "I'm getting hungry."

"Four more. I help cook."

"You strike a hard bargain, little dude." He stuck out his arm. "But it's a deal."

Liam shook Bill's hand. "Deal."

The guys from Damon's squad, Liam's honorary uncles, visited when they could, but over the past two years they'd dropped by less and less. Some attended professional development schools. Some went to Special Forces training. Some joined other military units. Some left the army. Their group of friends had gotten smaller, but Liam had never been this animated with them, people he'd known his entire life. He rarely acted this way with her. Only Peanut. Liam's one and only friend.

Though Bill Paulson could probably qualify as her son's friend now. The guy had the right touch with Liam.

Jealousy stabbed Grace, an unexpected emotion. One she didn't like.

So what if her son had a new friend? Bill was nothing more than a nice guy who'd offered them shelter for the night. Something she would expect from a man who rescued people for a living, but she hadn't imagined a bachelor being so in tune with a three-year-old.

Watching Bill and her son play together made her feel older than twenty-six. Sure, she got on the floor, and didn't mind a big mess with art projects or mud. But she was always so tired, as if she carried a hundred-pound pack all day, struggling to keep herself balanced and not fall over like one of those dominoes.

Unlike Bill. No tired eyes. No sagging shoulders. Only smiles and an innate strength she felt from the doorway.

She tucked her hair behind her ears. "Good morning."

Liam jumped to his feet and ran toward her. "Mommy."

The excitement in his voice warmed Grace's heart. This was more like it. She scooped him up, eager to have him in her arms. "I woke up, and you weren't in bed."

Liam gave her a wet kiss. "I wake up. Peanut, too. You asleep so I get Bill."

"You mean Mr. Paulson."

"That's my dad's name." Bill stood. "Liam can call me by my first name."

"Okay." She relented only because they would be leaving today. She cuddled her son close. Sniffed. "You smell like cookies."

Liam pointed to his new best friend. "Big dude."

Bill's cheeks reddened. "Liam wanted to wait until you were up to have breakfast, but we were a little hungry."

"Hungry men eat cookies." Liam spoke the words with a growly voice, as if mimicking someone.

Bill's entire face turned red. He cleared his throat. "Cookies have flour, eggs and milk in them. Not that different from pancakes."

"Cookies are healthy." Liam bent his arm to show off his biceps. "Make me strong. Like Bill."

Grace covered her mouth with her hand and bit back

laughter. "I can let cookies before breakfast slide this one time."

Bill's grin made him look more like one of Liam's peers than hers. "I appreciate that."

"It's the least I can do after being able to sleep in. That never happens." Or hadn't since Damon's final deployment. Grace was reminded of what she and Liam had lost in the mountains of Afghanistan, of what other people took for granted, without giving their good fortune a second thought. "I hope Liam didn't wake you up too early."

"I was awake when he knocked on my door. No reason for both of us to be up at the crack of dawn." Bill studied her with his watchful gaze. "I hope you weren't worried when he wasn't in bed."

She hugged Liam tight, remembering her fear waking up without him. He was all she had. "I had a moment of panic until I heard you in the kitchen."

Liam pushed away from her. "I winning."

Grace placed him on the floor. "You always win."

"And here I thought I had the age advantage," Bill joked. "Liam's quite the domino shark. He's kicking my bu—er, behind."

She appreciated the way Bill watched his language.

"I shark. Let's play," Liam shouted.

"Duty calls." Bill set up more dominoes. "Breakfast will have to wait a few more minutes."

"You boys play." Grace knew having a guy to play with was a big deal for her son. She'd let him have his fun. "I'll fix breakfast."

Bill's gaze met hers. "I don't mind cooking."

"Neither do I."

"You're a guest."

"And you're sweet." She meant each word. "Consider my cooking breakfast a bonus on top of the postcard I'll be sending."

He glanced at a waiting Liam, then back at her.

"Okay." He returned to setting up dominoes. "It's better this way. The guys at the station aren't that keen on my cooking."

"I find that hard to believe." He seemed like the kind of man who could do anything, including setting up dominoes while carrying on a conversation. "It's hard to ruin pancakes."

"Unless you burn them, turning breakfast into a three-alarm call."

"You're a firefighter," she said. "I'm sure you can take care of any flames."

"Oh, I know how to put out fires." He looked up with a mischievous grin. "I also know how to start them."

His words, flirtatious and suggestive, hung in the air. His gaze remained on her.

Grace's pulse skittered. Attraction buzzed all the way to her toes. Something passed between them. Something palpable. Something unsettling.

She looked away. Gulped.

"I have everything you need." He returned to the dominoes. "On the counter."

She opened her mouth to speak, but nothing came from her Mojave-dry throat. "Thanks," she finally said.

She shuffled to the kitchen in her bare feet, eager to put distance between them.

A few words from a gorgeous guy? A look? And she was incapacitated?

So not good.

Pancake mix sat on the counter, along with measuring cups, a wooden spoon, eggs and a stainless-steel bowl.

What was happening to her? She wasn't in shock. She didn't need more sleep. Maybe loneliness had finally sent her over the edge.

Grace measured the flour mixture. Her hand trembled and her vision blurred. She managed to fill the cup and dump the contents into the mixing bowl without making too much of a mess. She added water and eggs. Stirring the batter, she slowly regained her composure.

Dominoes clattered against the hardwood floor.

Liam laughed. "Oops."

Bill released a drawn-out sigh. "We'll have to try that again."

Her son clapped. "Again. Again."

"I've figured out your M.O.," their host said. "You don't do anything once."

Bill impressed Grace. "You pick up quick. Are you sure you aren't married with kids?" she asked him.

"Nope. Most of my friends are married, but my life is good, and I'm happy. Marriage and kids can wait until those things change. And if they don't change, then I'll be happily single."

"Wait until you meet the right woman."

"Why settle for one when there are so many out there?"

"So cavalier."

He shrugged. "Some of my friends have great marriages. Others not so good. My parents have struggled with a long-distance marriage."

Grace's life had started the day she fell in love with Damon. He'd wanted to spend the rest of his life with her, but being a Ranger kept him away from home and cut his life short. "Being married takes work whether you're together or not. Damon and I were apart a lot. Loving someone isn't easy. But we managed. Had a child. Were a family."

"My parents and I have never been much of a family. My dad is always away because of his job. His traveling is hard on my mom. Makes me wonder if the family thing is for me."

"If you don't know, it's good you're waiting to settle down."

"Thanks for saying that. Everyone else has been telling me to grow up because I'm missing out."

"I never said you weren't missing out," Grace teased.

She felt sorry for Bill. He could play all he wanted and be as sweet as could be, but she would never change places with him. At least she had Liam. One day, Bill was going to find himself lonelier than her.

"Cartoons. Cartoons," Liam chanted. "Peanut wants to watch cartoons."

Bill looked at her. "Is Liam allowed to watch TV?"

"Yes, but I limit how much."

"That's good," Bill said. "Kids should be outside playing and making snow angels, not sitting on the couch inside."

"You sure don't act like a confirmed bachelor who doesn't want kids."

"I may not want children of my own, but that doesn't mean I don't like other people's."

"Fair enough," she said. "You're the perfect playmate and babysitter rolled into one. If you ever get tired of being a firefighter, you'd make great manny."

His brow furrowed. "A what?"

"A male nanny."

He rose to his feet with the grace of an athlete. "I've been known to babysit a time or two. Though I'm the call of last resort."

That surprised her.

"Come on, little dude." He picked up Liam and grabbed Peanut. "You get the best seat in the house. My favorite chair."

Bill carried them into the living room. Thirty seconds later, the sound of cartoons filled the air. Liam squealed.

Her son seemed to like whatever Bill did. Of course, being a playmate or friend was easy. Being a parent and disciplinarian not so much.

Bill joined her in the kitchen. "How are the pancakes coming along?"

"Stirring the batter now."

"You've got a great kid."

"Thanks. But he has his moments."

"Don't we all."

Grace tried to focus on cooking, but curiosity about the handsome firefighter filled her mind with questions. "You said you don't plan on settling down any-time soon, but you must, um, date."

The second the words left her mouth she regretted them. Talk about awkward. But wanting to know more about him had gotten the best of her.

"Yeah, I do," he answered, as if she were asking if he put butter on his toast. "But I won't be dating again until December."

She added chocolate chips to the batter. "You don't look like the Grinch."

"I'm not. I love Christmas."

"Most people like having someone to date for the holidays."

"I'm not most people."

She would agree with that. "So why won't you date until after Christmas?"

"Too many family obligations."

"Do you have lots of brothers and sisters?"

"Just my mom and dad. I meant a date's family."

"You lost me."

"Nothing worse than being dragged to countless family gatherings, with everyone asking when's the wedding, even if you only started dating."

All she'd wanted to do while dating Damon was think and talk about their future. But she knew guys weren't like that. "That would get old."

"Didn't your family do that?"

"No, my family didn't want me getting serious with Damon. His family felt the same way."

"Why?"

"They thought we were too young. I was fifteen

when we started dating. Nineteen when we wed. My parents couldn't forgive me for eloping and marrying a man who'd joined the military instead of going to college. They haven't spoken to me since. Damon's folks were furious when he enlisted. They'd asked me to talk him out of it. Our getting married only made things worse."

"You'd think both sets of parents would be proud of what Damon was doing. The sacrifice he and you were making."

Bill had no idea how horrible both sets of parents had acted. "We made our choices. They made theirs."

He glanced around the doorway into the living room, then back at Grace. "Have you started dating again?"

Answering should be simple, but the unexpectedly personal question startled her. "A few months ago I went out with another Ranger."

"It didn't work out."

"He proposed. On the third date."

"Whoa."

"That's exactly what I thought." She poured batter onto the skillet. "Kyle is a sweet guy from Damon's platoon, but I wasn't sure if he was serious about marriage or trying to do the right thing by a fallen mate."

"Sounds like a good man, either way."

"He is, but…"

"But?"

She remembered Kyle, all earnest and sincere, proposing while Liam napped on the couch. She was all for being practical, but Kyle was a friend, nothing more. "I wasn't in love with him. We went on a few more dates, then it was time for him to deploy and…"

"Hard to go through that again."

"I wasn't going through it again." She hadn't been ready to marry another hero. She didn't want to love a man and give her all, but not be his priority.

God. Country. Army. Family.

That was how Damon's priorities fell. The army and serving a greater good had always come before her and Liam. She'd known where she'd fallen on the list going into the marriage, had accepted her place, respected it, because she was young, and her love for Damon was that strong.

But she was not about to accept being second, third or fourth again. Not for any man.

Grace and Liam deserved to be the number one priority. She would never settle for anything less.

"Breakfast was delicious." Sitting at the table, Bill leaned back in the chair, his stomach full and a satisfied smile on his face. He liked having a woman cook breakfast for him, especially one with sleep-rumpled hair, wearing his pajamas. The circles under Grace's eyes had faded. She must have slept well last night. That pleased him. "Thanks."

"You're welcome." Glancing out the window, she dragged her upper teeth over her bottom lip. "The snow is coming down hard."

"This morning's weather forecast predicts it will fall all day and into the night. A real bummer."

Her features tensed. "I'm sorry if we're in your way."

"You're not in the way." Bill annunciated each word. He needed to be careful what he said. Grace took things too personally. "I'm bummed the weather will keep me from skiing today. I have to be at the station early tomorrow morning, so I'll miss making first tracks in the freshies."

Grace gave him a blank stare.

"Powder," he clarified. "You don't ski."

"There are ski resorts in Iowa, but skiing wasn't something Damon and I ever tried."

Bill couldn't tell from her tone whether she was interested in the sport or not. "It's never too late to learn."

"I doubt there's a ski resort near Astoria."

Not interested. Too bad. Bet she would like skiing if she gave it a try. "No, but the mountain will always be here."

"Maybe when Liam is older."

"He's old enough now."

She stared at her son, who was picking chocolate chips out of his pancakes. "He's three."

Liam raised four fingers. "Almost four."

"That's the age I learned to ski."

"But you lived on the mountain." Grace's words rushed out. "I bet everyone in Hood Hamlet skis when they're in preschool."

Bill didn't know if she was trying to convince him or herself. "Many do, but lots of kids who don't live here learn to ski at a young age. The earlier, the better. That way there's no fear."

She shook her head. "Fear seems healthy, considering you're speeding down a mountain."

"Kids have a lower center of gravity and don't have as far to fall. Helmets protect them." Liam had chocolate and maple syrup smeared on his chin. Bill could count the number of family breakfasts he'd had, growing up, with both his mom and dad at the table. That was too bad because this was…nice. "Want me to teach you how to ski, little dude?"

Liam raised his hands in the air. "Ski…!"

Grace shook her head. "He doesn't know what skiing is."

"I'll show him."

"Maybe if we were staying—"

"Look out the window. You're not going anywhere."

"You can't go to the mountain today. Tomorrow you work."

Okay, she had a point. Bill shouldn't have offered to teach Liam to ski. He shouldn't have flirted with Grace before breakfast, either. He might find her attractive, but he didn't want her to think he was romantically interested in her.

"Just an idea." A bad one, except… Bill's dad might be alive, but he'd never been around long enough to show him how to do anything. Liam's father was dead. The kid was going to need someone to teach him about the outdoors and other guy stuff. "But who knows how long it'll take them to fix your truck."

Grace's lips parted, a combination of shock and panic. "I thought I could leave today."

Maybe Bill should have included denial in the mix. "Not in *this* weather."

"Once the storm passes…"

Damn. She had no idea about how long bodywork could take. Neither did he, but the vehicle wouldn't be ready today. "A claims adjustor from your insurance company needs to assess the damage before your truck can be repaired. Sometimes they don't have to do it in person, but other times they will."

Her head dropped slightly. She touched her forehead with both hands, rubbing her temples as if trying to put out a fire.

He wished she would relax. "Thad Humphreys owns the body shop. He's a good guy. A great mechanic. Talk to him before you start worrying."

Her hands froze. "Who says I'm worrying?"

She was the epitome of worry. Bill didn't like that. "No one."

Grace lowered her arms to her side. "I have a lot on my mind."

"I'm sure you do." He wanted to help her, but some things he couldn't do. "I hate to add to your list of things to do, but you should contact your insurance company and file a claim."

"I called them after Liam fell asleep last night. I didn't think you'd mind me using your phone."

Not a complete damsel in distress. "I don't."

"I wonder if they've towed the truck."

"Not yet."

Her shoulders slumped.

He didn't like seeing her so dejected. "I bet as soon as there's a break in the weather, they'll be right out."

Her mouth twisted.

"This isn't what you wanted to happen, but try to

enjoy yourself." He wished she didn't seem so concerned all the time. "Relax."

"I need to clean up the kitchen."

"The dishes can wait."

Someone needed to show Grace how to lighten up and have fun. Bill knew how to make that happen.

Not in his usual way.

He needed to get her on the mountain and fill her lungs with fresh air and put a smile on her face that would last longer than a blink. Too bad the weather wasn't cooperating.

"Snowman, snowman," Liam chanted.

"It's snowing too hard." Bill hated to disappoint the kid, but safety first. "We're going to have to stay inside for now."

Liam pouted.

"I'm sure we can find something else to do," Grace said.

Bill reviewed the options for kid fun inside his house. Not much beyond TV, Xbox and a few board games. And then he remembered. "I could use some help decorating my Christmas tree."

Liam bounced Peanut on the table. "Tree. Tree."

"He's in." Bill flashed Grace a charming grin. Not the one that encouraged beautiful, sexy women to type their numbers into his cell phone. The I'm-a-good-guy-you-can-trust-me grin he used on everybody else. "What about you?"

The look on her face made him think she was doing calculus in her head. "Uh, sure, but would it be okay if I took a shower first?"

Sexy images of bare skin, hot water and steam filled his head. He would like nothing better than to join her.

Bill swallowed. "Go ahead. I'll take care of the kitchen."

Grace rose. "My suitcase?"

"In the living room by the front door." He started clearing the table, leaving Liam to finish gorging himself on chocolate chips dipped in maple syrup. Two of Bill's favorite foods. "I didn't see any cracks in the shell last night. I went ahead and grabbed a couple of plastic bins from the back. One had a few toys in it."

"Thanks," she said. "The conditions must have been horrendous."

"I've been out in worse."

"With OMSAR?"

"In June, during a mission, my team had to spend the night in a snow cave."

"You must have been freezing."

"It was fun."

She studied him. "You like to have fun."

"Fun is the name of the game."

Having them here was fun. A different kind of fun than Bill was used to having, but he had no complaints. Even if nudity wasn't involved. Which it wouldn't be. Not with Grace. Only wholesome, kid-friendly fun. Still, he had a feeling he wouldn't have to worry about being bored.

That was good.

Bill carried more dishes to the counter.

His dad claimed boredom was the enemy. Bill hated being bored. He liked a variety of activities. One thing—an activity or a woman—never held his attention for long. Another reason why settling down held zero appeal.

His parents had celebrated their thirty-fifth wedding anniversary this year, but Bill wondered why his dad had gone the wife-and-kid-route in the first place. The man worked all over the globe, wherever his job in the oil industry took him. He never wanted to be home, had never wanted them to visit him on site. His dad never wanted them around, period.

Bill hated hearing his mom say he was like his father. He didn't want to be like his dad. Didn't want to break his wife's heart each time he left, and wasn't there when she needed him. He didn't want to break promises to his kid, who loved him more than anything. He didn't want his family to ever question whether he loved them back or not.

But he *was* like his father. Bill had failed his mother during her pregnancy. He'd failed helping Hannah after Nick died. He'd failed his best friend, Leanne, by not realizing she'd been spending her holidays alone.

Bill wouldn't get involved in a serious relationship.

He didn't want to fail and hurt another woman.

Not after seeing what his mom had gone through over the years, and was still going through when his dad was away.

Bill couldn't do that to a child.

Not after wondering if he'd done something to make his dad not want to be around.

No way. That wouldn't be fun or fair.

CHAPTER FOUR

"WINTER WONDERLAND" PLAYED on Bill's living room speakers. Light snow fell outside the wood-framed windows. Grace might as well be standing inside a snow globe. She knew exactly how the enclosed glass bubble world would feel. Cozy and comfortable and safe.

How she felt right now.

Unbelievable. Under the circumstances.

Bill dug through a big box. "There's an ornament in here you'll like, little dude."

"I'll help." Liam set Peanut on the floor.

At the breakfast table, the handsome firefighter had wanted her to relax. She'd figured that wasn't possible. Two hours later, she realized she'd been wrong. Grace half laughed.

Bill glanced her way. "You look more relaxed."

Someone could flip her make-believe world upside down to shake the snow, and still she knew today would be okay. An odd feeling, given the uncertainty over her truck. "Surprisingly, I am."

"Look at that, bud, your mom is chillin' in Hood Hamlet."

Liam grinned. "Chillin' Mommy."

"I can't remember the last time I *chilled,* but the Christmas spirit around here is contagious." Bill's faded jeans and blue henley shirt could easily be a red velvet Santa suit that matched the hat he wore. "I'm waiting for you to start ho-ho-hoing."

He put his hands on his flat stomach and leaned back. "Ho-ho-ho."

Liam burst out laughing.

Grace appreciated Bill's sense of humor. "How do you make everything so much fun?"

He shrugged. "It's a gift."

"A wonderful gift." Bill helped Grace focus on the present. Something she hadn't done in far too long. Humming along to the song, she hung a silver bell on the tree.

The branch bounced.

The bell rang. The chime lingered on the fir-scented air.

Arms outstretched, Liam ran to the front door, where a two-inch-wide red leather strap with four gold bells hung from the doorknob. He pulled on the strap, ringing them.

Bill sang the chorus from "Jingle Bells."

Grace joined in.

The singing invigorated Liam. With each shake, his impish grin widened. He bounced from foot to foot, excited and offbeat.

The song ended, but Liam didn't stop ringing the bells. If he had pointy ears and shoes, he would make the perfect elf to Bill's Santa. The thought blanketed her heart with warmth.

She adjusted a silver ball on the tree. "The jingling makes me think of a horse-drawn sleigh."

Bill gave Liam a thumbs-up. "Ever been on one?" he asked her.

"No, but I saw one in a Hallmark Christmas movie on TV."

Liam's ringing went on and on and on.

Grinning, Bill shook his head. "The little dude likes the bells."

"Liam loves all types of bells." She motioned her son back to the tree. "I'll hang the strap somewhere out of reach."

"Don't. The front door is perfect." Bill's gaze traveled from the miniature village on the end table, past a clock on the wall that played carols on the hour, over a stuffed Christmas moose on the entertainment unit to a nativity scene set on the mantel. "Thanks for putting out the decorations. The house is ready for Santa."

Memories of a revolving iridescent tree that changed colors rushed back. Her mom had loved anything unique when it came to Christmas. The more bizarre the decoration, the better. But Grace had been uninvited from all holidays, her cards and presents returned unopened the year she'd married Damon.

Grace preferred rustic and homespun decor, like the kind she'd found in the additional boxes of Christmas decorations Bill had brought out. She'd had a blast finding spots for each item. She couldn't wait for him to see his snowman-themed guest bath or his candy-cane kitchen. "You're welcome, but decorating was my pleasure."

She'd made halfhearted attempts to make Christmas special for Liam, but he'd been too young to know what was happening, and she'd felt so alone after Damon died. But today was different.

After years of apartment living, she'd dreamed about spending Christmas in a house, decking the halls and trimming a real tree. Only today was no dream. Everything was real, from sitting around the table eating breakfast like a family, to spending the day with Bill, who was proving to be…well, maybe a little too perfect.

The perfect host, anyway.

No man was perfect.

A guy like Bill, a first responder and hero, someone who risked his life and put the needs of others ahead of his own family, was far from Grace's idea of Mr. Right. If she were interested in finding Mr. Right.

She wasn't.

Maybe after she made a life for herself in Astoria, and Liam was older. But she had no reason to be thinking about that now.

Time to embrace the feeling of family and enjoy the glad tidings tied up in a shiny ribbon. Maybe this would be the start of a new tradition for her and Liam.

She'd never seen him happier.

"Look at this." Bill showed Liam an ornament. "My dad gave me this fire engine when I told him I wanted to be a firefighter. It's one of my favorites. Put it on the tree for me."

Liam's mouth formed an O.

Bill handed over the ornament.

Her son held the miniature fire truck as he would a priceless treasure.

"Find an empty branch," Bill encouraged.

Liam scanned the tall tree. He raised his arm toward a bare branch, but came four inches short. The ornament dangled from his little fingers.

Grace's heart lurched. If he let go…

Liam rose on his tiptoes.

She held her breath.

Bill's smile didn't waver. "Almost there, buddy."

He didn't sound concerned at all.

She nibbled a fingernail.

The tip of Liam's tongue stuck out between his lips. He stretched again, but fell short. Dropping onto his heels, he puckered his lips.

Bill rubbed his whisker-covered chin. Liam hadn't given the guy time to shower this morning, let alone shave.

The stubble gave Bill a dangerous edge. She wondered if the whiskers would scratch her face if he kissed her. Not that she wanted to be kissed by him. Or anybody else.

"That's a good branch you picked out, but why stop there?" Bill asked. "Help me put the fire truck toward the top."

Liam nodded, his eyes twinkling with excitement.

Bill lifted him into the air.

"Higher," Liam commanded, then giggled.

With a whoop and a holler, Bill obliged.

Liam beamed like the brightest star in the sky on Christmas Eve.

Grace placed her hand over her thrumming heart. She loved seeing her son so happy. They both needed to laugh more. That would be one of her New Year's resolutions.

Liam pointed at her. "Mommy's turn. Lift her up."

Heat rushed up her neck. "I'm too heavy."

Setting Liam on the ground, Bill grinned wryly. "You're not even close to being too heavy."

Liam grabbed a Nutcracker ballerina from the box and handed the ornament to her. "Go on, Mommy. Lots of empty branches up top."

The thought of Bill's large, warm hands around her waist made Grace want to fan herself. He could make her skin dance and her blood boil with a simple touch. But she shouldn't. She couldn't. "Thanks, but I wouldn't want you to hurt your back."

"Remember, all those green fruits and veggies made me strong." Bill's voice lowered to a deep and oh-so-sexy tone. "I can handle you."

Her heart tripped. "I'm not sure I can handle *you*."

He raised a brow. "You never know unless you try."

Temptation flared. Grace loved a challenge. That was how she'd ended up dating Damon back in high school. But she was no longer a teenager caught up in that first blush of love.

This morning, the line between daydreams and reality was blurring. Grace couldn't be reckless with her heart. She couldn't be reckless with Liam. She had to be careful. Not douse the spark waiting to ignite inside her with a full container of lighter fluid.

She raised her chin, meeting Bill's gaze straight on. "I could try, but it's not worth the risk. What if you're wrong and throw your back out? You won't be able to finish decorating the tree, or make a snowman if the weather improves, or go to work in the morning."

She and her son had never experienced this kind of family time preparing for the holidays. Having Bill a part of it was special. No sense letting fear ruin the day for Liam.

Bill studied her. "You're practical."

Grace expected to hear teasing in his voice, not… respect. "Being practical goes with being a mom."

Bill swept Liam into the air again. "You're a lucky guy to have such a great mom."

Her heart went pitter-pat like the Little Drummer Boy's stick against his drum. Her life revolved around being Liam's mom. There was no better compliment. "Thanks."

Holding on to a glittery green ball, Liam nodded. "Best mommy ever."

Grace's chest tightened. All she'd ever wanted to be was a great mom. A great wife, too. Maybe someday she'd get another chance at the latter. "You're the best son ever."

Liam nodded. "And Bill best daddy."

The word *daddy* floated on the air, a comic strip dialogue bubble looming over Bill's head.

Her joy evaporated. Her stomach churned. Her heart hurt. He was going to burst Liam's bubble and…

Bill casually ruffled her son's hair. "That's the nicest thing anyone's ever said to me, little dude. Where do you want to hang the ball?"

Grace released the breath she'd been holding.

Liam pointed to one of the upper branches. "There."

"You've got this." Bill lifted him higher.

Her son hooked the ornament on the tree and was lowered to the floor. He dived into the box of ornaments. "More. More."

"Let's put them all on," Bill said.

Maybe she'd overreacted, hearing Liam call another man Daddy. Maybe she'd been the only one feeling uncomfortable. Maybe Bill could smooth over an awkward moment like buttercream icing on a wedding cake.

A *wedding* cake?

Her insides trembled.

Maybe she'd better forget this holiday fun and run as far away from Bill as she could during the next break in the storm. Not that she had a way to leave besides her two feet. Darn it.

Grace could count on one hand the times Liam had said the word *daddy*. He didn't remember his father. He'd been too young. But she told him stories about Damon and showed him pictures. Liam had seen other kids and their daddies at preschool and at the college day care where he'd stayed while she attended classes.

Guess he thought Bill looked like a daddy.

A superhot daddy.

Don't go there.

Getting her son a daddy wasn't on her to-do list. Or her Christmas list.

Bill Paulson was not the answer to their prayers. He was not going to wrap himself up in a big bow. He was a one-day savior, not a long-term one.

Not that Grace needed saving.

She needed to get a grip on her fantasies and kick him out of the starring role.

He touched her shoulder. "You okay?"

Grace startled. No, she wasn't okay, but she nodded, not wanting to admit the truth. She needed to protect her son's heart. How was she going to do that? And protect herself, too.

She glanced out the window. Still snowing. That meant she was stuck here with Liam's idea of a daddy. And Bill happily acting the part.

His eyes didn't let go. "You look miles away."

She wished she was miles away. Away from him and the sugarplum temptation of his make-believe world, where all was safe and perfect.

Grace, of all people, knew better.

She gave her head a hard shake. "Just thinking."

"About me?" he teased.

Her cheeks flamed. If he only knew…

He made her feel things she'd buried deep inside her when she'd laid her husband to rest at Arlington. She would rather face a roomful of black widow spiders than tell him the truth.

"About today." Which was true. "I've never decorated a live Christmas tree before. They sell them, but we used an artificial one."

"Then we're even. I've never decorated a fake tree."

"I can't imagine buying a fake tree when your backyard is a forest."

"True, but most of the trees outside are too big for in here. I applied for a permit to cut this one down. I do that every year."

"Of course you did." She didn't hesitate a moment. "You follow the rules."

He glanced at Liam, who lay on the floor flying an angel ornament in the air, then back at her. Bill's mouth curved into an inviting you-know-you-want-me smile. "Depends on the rule."

Enough charm and sensuality infused his words to ignite a ball of heat in her belly.

Not good, Grace. Not good at all.

Her mouth went dry. Her mind raced, imagining what rules he'd broken, where and how. And with whom.

She tried hard to be good, to do what was right. Would she ever have the chance to do something… naughty, or was she stuck being nice?

Liam handed her an angel ornament. "Here, Mommy."

"Thanks, sweetie." Grace focused her attention on the angel with feather wings and a gold pipe-cleaner halo, over the picture of a little girl's face. "Who is this?"

"Kendall Bishop-Willingham." The tender smile on Bill's face suggested Kendall was someone special. "She's the daughter of my friends Hannah and Garrett."

"Beautiful."

Bill nodded. "Each year Kendall and her two younger brothers give me ornaments. Without them I'd have nothing but round balls and bells."

Liam ran to the door and jingled the bells. The sound got louder and louder until she couldn't hear the Christmas carols playing.

Bill shook his head with a laugh. "I said the magic word."

"Bells," she and Bill shouted at the same time.

Liam danced. He rang the bells again.

Her gaze met Bill's. Something passed between them, the same connection she'd experienced last night.

She wanted to look away, but couldn't.

He seemed in no hurry, either.

A bell-size lump formed in her throat.

"More. More." Liam's chant broke the spell. "Need to decorate."

For the best. Common sense told Grace that, yet a part of her wished the connection could have continued. She inhaled deeply and looked to her son.

Liam pulled a red ball from the ornament box. "Up. I want to put on this one."

"Sure thing, buddy." Bill raised her son into the air again. "By the time we're finished with the tree, I won't need a workout."

Bill sounded so content. Nothing seemed to bother him, except not being able to ski. This must be what an always-up-for-a-good-time kind of guy was like.

What would he think if she told him she hadn't been to a gym in nearly three years? Or hadn't eaten a meal with another adult in two months, until last night?

Their worlds were so different. She kept forgetting that when she was with him.

Grace hung the angel on the tree.

She couldn't imagine having Bill's carefree life. She worked hard, paid her bills, cared for her son, cooked and cleaned. After that? No time. No energy. No sleep. Nothing left for her.

"Look, Mommy." Liam hung the red ball on the tree. "Shiny and pretty like you."

Her affection for him overflowed.

Liam meant everything to her.

Unlike Bill's, her life wasn't perfect. Her heart was missing a huge chunk. Her faith was battered. Her nights were lonely. But she had her son. He was all she needed. Anything—anyone—else would be a bonus, an indulgence, like whipped cream on ice cream, and a cherry on top.

Moving away from the tree, Bill brushed her shoulder with his arm. "Sorry."

Her pulse skittered. Heat emanated from the point of contact. Grace took a calming breath. It didn't help.

Forget bonuses. Whipped cream was full of calories and fat. No need for indulgences. maraschino cherries were sticky, full of chemicals and food coloring.

She glanced at the handsome firefighter.

Totally unnecessary. Bad for her.

And to be avoided at all costs.

After lunch, Bill stood next to the six-foot snowman in his front yard. He had summited Denali, scaled peaks in Patagonia, skied in Chamonix. He enjoyed vacations that pushed him to the physical limits, whether on another continent or here on Mount Hood. Building a snowman with Grace and Liam was the last thing he'd expected to be doing on his day off. Surprisingly, it didn't suck.

Snowflakes fell from the sky, much lighter than the blanket of white that had poured down earlier. The sharp scent of pine tickled his nose. His breath hung in the air. Familiar sights and smells, until he looked at his house and saw a blue elephant sitting on the living room windowsill.

Not so typical.

His childhood memories of snow days revolved around playing with his friends. Today was Bill's first experience of family time in the snow, the kind of day he'd always wanted to spend with his parents when he was a kid. But his dad had always been away, or too busy when he was home. His mom had been game for about thirty minutes, until she thought the temperature was too cold.

Bill enjoyed this afternoon's interlude from reality more than he thought he would. He'd liked being called Daddy, and liked having the kid look up to him. For a few hours, Bill could be the kind of father he wished his dad had been. And no one would be hurt when he went back to being a fun-loving, womanizing bachelor. A win-win for all involved.

Liam stuck out his tongue, trying to catch a snowflake.

Grace held up a camera. She wore one of his soft shell jackets over her zip-up fleece. Strands of brown hair stuck out from under the colorful stripped wool beanie, also his. A pair of black gloves kept her hands warm. She looked wintery cute, like a photo from a Hood Hamlet Visitors Center brochure.

"Got it." She focused the lens on Bill. "Your turn."

He struck a serious pose, if pretending to be an artist sculpting snow could be deemed serious.

Liam jumped into the picture. Not easy with knee-high snow and so many articles of clothing he looked like the Michelin Man. The poor kid had to be sweating beneath all the layers Grace had made him wear.

The condensation from her sigh floated away on the air.

Bill had to laugh. "Photo bomb."

"I don't think he knows what that is." She lowered her camera. The cold had turned her cheeks rosy. Her eyes were clear and bright. "At least I hope not."

"Then the kid's a natural." Bill patted Liam's fleece cap. "Because he's got the method down."

"It's nice to see him clown around."

Grace's lighthearted tone thrilled Bill. Emptying her pickup and watching the truck be towed away had seemed to release the remaining grip she held on herself after decorating the tree.

Bad stuff happened.

Life went on.

Now she was smiling. Singing Christmas carols. Playing.

He couldn't be happier.

Liam tugged on Bill's arm. "Frosty needs nose."

"Yes, he does." Bill looked around. "I brought out a carrot."

"Abra-dabra." The kid pulled one arm from behind his back. He clutched the carrot in his mitten-covered hand. "One nose."

"Nice trick, little dude." Bill gave a thumbs-up. "You'll have to teach me that later."

Grace positioned herself to take a picture. "Be careful."

Bill rolled his eyes. Mothers could caution, but kids needed to be kids. Get into scraps, jams and fights. Knock over a snowman or two.

"Liam's so padded he looks like he's wearing bubble wrap," Bill said. "He'll be fine if he falls."

The kid might even bounce.

"Liam's not used to snow." Her mouth tightened. "You've worked hard on the snowman. He could fall on top of it."

She didn't seem used to the white stuff, either.

"Snow is soft. More forgiving than grass. And snowmen have short life expectancies." Bill held out his arms. "Come on, bud. Frosty needs his nose."

Liam flew into them. With so many layers, Bill couldn't feel the little body underneath. It was like holding on to a stuffed animal.

Grace snapped more pictures. The kid stuck in the carrot.

"That's much better."

The click of the camera continued.

"Good job." Bill released Liam. "Does Frosty need anything else?"

The kid studied the snowman like an art dealer appraising a van Gogh. "Frosty good."

She took another picture. "Awesome."

The darkening sky told Bill more snow was on the way. Best to make the most of the reprieve from the storm. "Time to make snow angels."

"Snow angels?" Liam's scarf muffled the words.

Grace stepped forward. "Georgia Christmases are more green than white. We've never done that before."

"Then it's a good thing you came to Hood Hamlet, because we always have white Christmases." Bill held Liam's hand. Bill's dad never taught him to do anything outdoors. It had been his mom, then Nick and Jake. "I grew up making angels. I'll show you how."

Bill walked to a canvas of fresh snow in front of a semicircle of tall pines. He released Liam's hand. "Do you know how to do a jumping jack?"

Liam did five.

"That's all you have to do, except you're not standing up." Bill lay on the snow with his arms extended. The cold seeped into him, a familiar feeling. "Get down like this, then do a jumping jack."

He flapped his arms up and down, scissored his legs in and out, flattening the snow on either side of his body. He carefully rose, then motioned to his creation. "Look what I made."

"Angel. Angel." Liam's eyes widened. "I want to make one."

"You can make as many as you want." Bill looked at Grace. "Trigger finger ready?"

She positioned her camera. "The first one is going on video."

"Start here, bud." Bill pointed to a patch of snow. "Lie down."

Liam did.

Bill talked him through the steps.

The padding of winter clothing hampered the boy's movements, but he didn't give up. The grin on his face grew with each sweep of snow. Giggles filled the air.

Bill clapped, his gloves muting the sound. Playing with Liam and making Grace smile was like a siren's call, but no matter how seductive, he wasn't ready for a family long-term. He would end up blowing it just as his dad kept doing. Bill needed to hold on to reality. His reality. "You're an expert angel-making boy."

"Again. Again."

"Let me help you up so you can make another." He held out his arm and pulled Liam to his feet, then glanced at Grace. "I'm going to have a yardful of angel Liams."

"He doesn't—"

"It's fine." Bill aimed a disarming smile in her direction. One he hoped told her she could relax. All was well. And would remain that way today.

Liam fell on his butt. Instead of standing, he made an angel right there.

Grace snapped a picture.

Bill motioned to a fresh patch of snow. "Give me the camera. I want to see you make a snow angel."

She just clutched it tighter. "I'm taking pictures so I can make a scrapbook page."

"Capturing memories is good, but making them is better."

Her nose scrunched. "I like both kinds."

"You make the angel. I'll take the pictures."

She gripped the camera. "I don't—"

"Mommy angel." Liam was covered in snow and smiling. "Mommy needs to make an angel."

Her mouth quirked.

Way to go, little dude.

Grace was trapped.

About time.

Bill couldn't get her up in the tree this morning, but he'd damn well get her down in the snow now.

Come on, Gracie. Let go. Show me what you're made of.

CHAPTER FIVE

MORE SNOW FELL from the sky, bigger flakes than before. Bill extended his arm toward Grace. "I'll make sure I get this on video, too."

She gave up her camera, then stuck out her tongue.

He focused the lens on her. "Do that again."

She feigned innocence, raising her hands in the air, palms up. "Do what?"

Grace Wilcox had a devilish side. That intrigued him. A good thing she wasn't going to be here long or he might do something he would regret. "Make your snow angel."

"I'm going to get all wet."

Oh, boy. He could have fun with that line. But he wouldn't. He couldn't with Liam within earshot. Bill would watch out for the kid the way he wished his dad would have cared for him. That was the least he could do until the two Wilcoxes left Hood Hamlet. "It's only water. You'll dry."

See? He could be good. Even though he would rather be bad.

"Last night you were worried about hypothermia," she said.

"Today I'm not." He hit the record button on the video mode. "Show your mom what to do."

Liam instructed her with enthusiasm. The two made a set of mother-and-son figures, then another and another. Snow covered them until they looked like yetis from the Himalayas. Happy ones. Smiling ones.

That pleased Bill.

He filmed them and took pictures. She would have memories for her book or wall. A few to tuck away in her heart. He would have some, too. Memories were all he could afford from this time with them. No matter how much he was enjoying himself. A day or two of being a family guy was his limit. At least that was how long his dad could last at home.

"Enough angel making for me." Grace stood, brushing the snow off front and backside.

Bill enjoyed the show, then handed her the camera. "I only cut your head off in a few shots."

She made a face.

He raised his hands. "Kidding."

Liam made his way toward them.

"Are you ever serious?" she asked.

Oh, Bill could be very serious, especially in the horizontal position. "Sometimes when I'm on a call or a mission."

"Only sometimes?"

"Life's short. It's meant to be enjoyed. Let's just say I'm glad you knocked on my door."

"Us, too." Grace walked to the three-feet-tall Santa decoration with a lightbulb inside the molded plastic figure. She brushed off the light cover of snow. "The least I can do is clean up this jolly fellow, who showed us the way to your house."

Liam threw snowballs at Frosty.

Bill joined her on that side of the yard. "What do you mean?"

"It was so dark and snowy I couldn't see anything, until I glimpsed Santa glowing like a lighthouse."

"I put him out in the yard yesterday."

"Lucky timing."

Of course someone not from around here would chalk up good fortune to luck, but he knew better. "Not luck. Christmas magic."

"Right. Flying reindeers and dancing elves."

He recognized the doubt in her eyes. "You mock, but Christmas magic exists in Hood Hamlet. I've seen it myself. Things happen on the mountain this time of year—accidents, lost climbers—that should end in tragedy but end happily instead. Even my skeptical best friend, Leanne, now believes."

Grace's forehead creased. "Your best friend is a woman?"

He nodded. "Since we were nine."

"What changed your friend's mind?"

"Love."

Grace straightened.

That had gotten her attention. But not surprising. Women wanted to find love.

"Leanne is getting married on Saturday. Her gift is under the tree," Bill stated.

"Falling in love? Getting engaged? Those things changed her mind?"

He nodded. "Christmas magic is a big deal around here. The town's second annual Christmas Magic Festival was held on Saturday."

"Guess the magic kept the snow away until Sunday so the celebration could go on."

"It sure did," he said. "Maybe Christmas magic brought you to Hood Hamlet last night."

"Maybe." She spoke with a wistful expression on her face. "Or maybe it was an angel."

"Christmas is a time for miracles, but I haven't had much experience with angels except the snow kind," Bill said. "I'll stick with magic."

"You do that." She glanced at Liam. "I'm going to stick with my angel the next time I need a Christmas miracle."

Bill wouldn't mind sticking with *her*.

Whoa. Where had that come from?

He wasn't up for sticking with anyone. Not for more than a night. Maybe two if they had fun together.

Maybe the temperature had dropped more than he realized. Time to head inside and warm up. He was thinking nonsense right now. "The snow's picking up. Let's warm up inside and make ourselves some hot cocoa. We can check if there's an update on your truck."

Her soft smile kicked his gut with the force of an ornery mountain goat. He made himself breathe.

Something was at work here. Not magic. Physical chemistry.

That would explain the way he felt. But he couldn't

fool around with Grace no matter how appealing the thought might be.

"You're a good guy, Bill Paulson."

"Thanks."

He'd been good all day, but his bad boy side wanted to come out and play with Grace.

Standing in Bill's kitchen, Grace adjusted the phone receiver to better hear Thad Humphreys, the owner of the Hood Hamlet Garage and Body Shop. She was having trouble concentrating on what he was saying. Her fingers stung from the ice that had slipped into her gloves while outside playing. Her mind whirled from the fun she'd had with Bill.

She needed a break, some distance from him.

The guy was charming and handsome and oh so sweet to her son. She'd found herself wishing Christmas magic could be true, and maybe she'd get something special—maybe someone special—from Santa this year. Silly. A few hours of fun didn't change anything.

"Your truck has over one hundred eighty thousand miles on it," Thad said. "The damage from the collision is pretty significant, plus the engine is shot. The claims adjustor will likely total the vehicle."

Air rushed from her lungs. Hands trembling, she clutched the phone receiver. "Total it?"

"Yeah, I'm sorry. But there's a way you can still keep the truck if you don't want to buy a new one."

Buy a new one. The words added a hundred pounds

of weight to each of her shoulders. Shoulders that hadn't felt burdened thirty minutes ago.

"I just wanted to give you a heads-up," Thad said.

Grace wanted to hang up, go back to playing outside and trying not to notice how blue Bill's eyes were when the light hit them right. But she knew that wasn't possible. There was no going back.

She swallowed around the snowball-size lump in her throat. "Thanks."

"I'm sure this isn't what you expected to hear."

"No."

"I'm happy to discuss your options. But think about whether you want to fix the truck or buy a new one." Sympathy filled Thad's voice. Who better than a mechanic to understand the sentimental attachment to a vehicle? "The claims adjustor isn't available until Wednesday. You have a couple of days to decide."

Wednesday. Two days from now.

She tightened her grasp on the phone. "Okay. Thanks. Goodbye."

Grace disconnected from the call, placed the phone in its charger, slumped against the refrigerator.

Where would she stay? What would she do about the truck that had meant the world to Damon?

She blinked, not wanting to cry.

Laughter floated into the kitchen from the living room. She'd learned good times didn't last. Another lesson she'd forgotten in this house until Thad's phone call. At least Liam sounded happy. That made one of them.

She leaned against the kitchen counter, her usual source for support.

Two days to make a decision.

She'd spent a year debating whether to leave Columbus or not. Months deciding where to go. Weeks selling furniture and books and clothes and baby gear so she could fit all she had into Damon's truck.

A truck not worth repairing.

It's going to be okay, babe.

No, it wasn't.

Goose bumps covered her arms, ones that had nothing to do with the cold.

The truck had been Damon's most treasured possession. Selling his other things had been bearable because the truck was the only thing that mattered to him. He'd purchased the vehicle his senior year of high school from a local farmer, after doing maintenance on it for years. He loved working on the truck, keeping the vehicle in running order. She'd never had to worry about having mechanical problems. But the old truck's performance had suffered without Damon's TLC.

Along with everything else.

Grace had no idea what another truck might cost, or if she needed a pickup at all. Except how would she get their stuff to Astoria in a car?

Damon had trusted her to make decisions, whether he was home or away. But he'd always been an email or Skype conversation away when she needed input. Now every decision she'd made since burying her husband filled her with doubts.

Her stomach churned.

Was she doing the right thing?

Should she get rid of the truck?

Could she let it go?

She had no one to turn to for advice. Except Bill, whose greatest concern was what woman he would kiss at midnight on New Year's Eve. Okay, that wasn't fair.

Grace blew out a puff of air. She would figure this out on her own. The way she always did.

She straightened, tucked her hair behind her ears, then walked into the living room.

Bill was crawling on his hands and knees. Liam sat on his back, giggling and full of excitement.

Not even the truck crisis could keep a smile away. "What is going on?"

"I cowboy. This is my horse." Liam held on to Bill's shirt collar. "Giddy-up, horsey."

Bill trotted across the floor like an obedient pony. Back and forth he moved, adjusting his speed based on his rider's commands.

Grace watched in wonder. Bill was going above and beyond, even for a nice guy. And her son was enjoying it greatly. Liam didn't remember being in his daddy's arms or in a baby pack against Damon's chest. "How did you get roped into being a horse?"

Looking at her, Bill neighed.

The guy was too much. "I didn't get that."

Liam made a face at her. "A horsey can't talk, Mommy!"

"Oh, I forgot." She wrung her hands, full of nervous energy. "Well, have fun. Looks like we're going to be in Hood Hamlet a few more days. I'm going to find us a place to stay so we can get out of your horse's hair."

Bill stopped crawling. "The truck."

Grace rubbed the back of her tight neck. She tilted her head toward Liam. "Maybe we can talk later. Things are sort of a mess."

Bill's gaze met hers, a sympathetic glance that told her he understood. "You're welcome to stay here as long as you're in Hood Hamlet."

A lump formed in her throat. "I—"

"Here. Here," her son chanted. "I want to stay with big dude."

Bill raised an eyebrow. "Liam thinks staying here is a good idea."

She swallowed. "Liam also thinks filling the toilet with a squad of toy soldiers is fun."

Bill glanced over his shoulder. "Don't do that here, bud, okay?"

"Okay," Liam said.

Bill looked back at her. "We're good."

Grace wasn't so sure. Liam hadn't left Bill's side all day. Dominoes. Breakfast. Tree trimming. Lunch. Playing in the snow. Horsey. The kid treated him like a wind-up plaything, and Bill was more than happy to oblige. Spending more time here might hurt Liam when they left for Astoria.

Her son had been too young to remember Damon leaving and not coming home, but he might be old enough to remember Bill. "Thanks, but you don't need us hanging around. You must have stuff to do."

"Not in this weather. The only thing on my agenda is work tomorrow."

"What if it keeps snowing?" she asked.

"Nothing keeps a firefighter away from the job. I have a four-wheel drive truck with a plow on the front. I work a twenty-four hour shift. This place will be all yours."

Her mouth fell open. "You trust us here alone?"

Bill's appreciative gaze raked over her, sending chills down her spine, the good kind, ones she hadn't felt in a very long time.

"You don't look like the type to take advantage of anyone."

Of course not. She looked like a frazzled mom trying to care for a curious three-year-old, with nowhere to go and no vehicle to take them there. But something about Bill's easygoing tone challenged her. She raised her chin. "Looks can be deceiving."

His brows slanted. "Got some crimes to confess?"

She tapped her finger against her chin. "Do you think I'd tell you if I did?"

The connection between them flared, stronger than ever. Hot, inviting, oh so tempting.

Crush. A foolish crush.

Self-preservation called for her retreat. But Grace couldn't stop staring. She didn't blink. She didn't move. She stood mesmerized.

Bill looked away first, but Grace didn't feel as if she'd won. He was only keeping her guessing.

His casual shrug belied his darkening eyes. "Doesn't matter to me if you have some deep dark secrets. All I have here is stuff."

She glanced around, trying to calm her rapid pulse.

A glass of ice water might cool her off. Or she could step outside. "Nice stuff."

"Replaceable." A faraway look filled his eyes. "People don't understand. When there's a fire they lose their minds over how this is gone or that is ruined. Sometimes we have to hold people back or pull them out of burning buildings over stuff. I get that it's hard to lose pictures and mementos, but nothing's worth saving except loved ones."

"You've seen some bad things."

He glanced over his shoulder at Liam once more. "Occupational hazard."

"I can't imagine."

"Don't." He spoke sharply, then his features relaxed into a smile. "Life is too precious to dwell on the negative stuff."

"You seem to have no problem focusing on the positive."

"Only way to go." He crawled across the floor with Liam on his back. "I bet the little dude makes it easy for you to do the same."

"Yes." Though not always.

Maybe she should follow Bill's advice. Expecting something to go wrong wasn't a good way to live. It wasn't how she and Damon had lived before that final deployment.

"So you'll stay?"

A "no" sat poised at the tip of her tongue. Thinking positively was one thing. Buying trouble was another. Something told her Bill Paulson could be big trouble. Her lips parted—

"Before you say no, hear me out." He moved closer. "Giving you a place to stay is the least I can do. It's my way of saying thank you for the sacrifices your family has made for our country."

Liam raised his arms and cheered. "Stay. Stay with Bill."

Holding on to the boy, Bill reared like a stallion, graceful and wild. Smiling like a fiend.

Grace tapped her fingers against her lips. "It could be a couple of days or longer. Thad thinks, um, things shouldn't be fixed."

Liam slid off Bill's back. Both stood.

"All the more reason to stay." Bill spoke as if this was nothing more than a weekend sleepover where they'd watch DVDs and eat popcorn and candy. "Don't waste money on a hotel when you have a free place here. Liam needs a Christmas tree and room to play. I have both."

Not to mention an adult-size playmate.

Liam nodded, as if he understood what Bill was saying.

"I won't be around much," he continued. "After my shift, I'm off for forty-eight hours. I spend most of that time on the mountain. Trust me, I won't be a good host."

"That's hard to believe. You've been amazing."

"You're easy to please, Grace." He looked down at his legs being hugged by Liam. "You, too, cowboy."

Bill's schedule alleviated her fears about Liam getting too attached. She had money, thanks to insurance and military benefits, but she wanted to be frugal. Still, she hesitated. "But Christmas is coming...."

"Let's take it a day at a time."

Both Liam and Bill were looking at her, waiting for her to decide. She couldn't think of any reason not to stay, but found herself balking. Bill rattled her nerves.

Liam tilted his head. "Puh-lease, Mommy."

"Listen to the kid," Bill said.

"If we stay, I don't want to be treated as a guest. I'll buy groceries. Cook. Clean."

"Not necessary."

She was outnumbered, but not about to give in. "Not negotiable."

"Then it's a deal." Bill held his hand up to her son. "Looks like you're staying, little dude."

Liam high-fived his new playmate. "Yay!"

"Nothing like Hood Hamlet in December." Bill shot her a sideways glance, making her pulse jump. "You won't regret this."

Grace hoped not. She'd lived with enough regrets. She didn't want to have to live with any more.

The next morning Bill entered the station stifling a yawn. The smell of freshly brewed coffee filled the air. He needed caffeine pronto. The little dude hadn't slept well last night. No one else in the house had, either.

That was what he got for telling Grace to stay. He didn't regret the invitation, though he'd given her little choice.

Why *had* he worked so hard to convince her? Why did it matter where she went?

He'd never thought the whole family thing was attractive, but something about spending more time with Grace and Liam had sucked him in. His common sense had fled or maybe gone into hibernation.

He crossed the apparatus bay, his steps echoing against the concrete floor, not another soul in sight. Everyone must be waiting for morning briefing from the chief. Bill hoped someone had brought breakfast. This morning he'd wanted to leave his house as quietly as possible, so hadn't grabbed any food.

A bad move according to his grumbling stomach.

Grace would agree and tell him breakfast was the most important meal of the day. Too bad they couldn't have eaten together.

Weird how he couldn't stop thinking about her.

Bill had tried to help last night, but his presence had been only a hindrance in getting Liam back to sleep. The little dude had wailed like a banshee with him around. So much for being good with kids.

He'd retreated to his room, trying not to think of having an after midnight play session with Grace. Hot, heavy fun. He was good at that. But…

Grace + Liam = off-limits.

Bill couldn't forget that, even if math had never been his best subject.

He headed toward the living quarters, basic but comfortable with a television area, large dining room and kitchen. The bunkrooms were upstairs, along with the bathrooms.

Bill hoped Grace and Liam were still asleep. She

had to be tired. He didn't know how she handled being a single parent. Not that she had a choice. At least his dad flew home a couple times a year, around major holidays. That had to count for something, right? Grace had no one. Not even parents she could call.

Maybe she could nap today. A vision of her in bed made him grin.

Bill pushed through the door. An argument about the upcoming Seattle Seahawks game on Sunday raised the decibels by a factor of two. A heated debate over the best local ski area—Timberline, Mount Hood Meadows or Ski Bowl—for fresh powder ensued. Two men bragged about the hot babes they'd bagged the other night. No doubt one of the guys was Riley Hansen.

In the dining room, both B and C shifts sat around the table. Every person had a coffee cup in hand. Three pink boxes of doughnuts and a stack of napkins rested in the center of the table. A typical morning at shift change.

"Good morning, fellows. And Thomas." Bill nodded toward his best friend, Leanne Thomas, who worked with him on C shift.

She sat next to her fiancé, Christian Welton, who had been moved by the chief to B shift after the engagement was made public. Leanne held an old-fashioned glazed doughnut. "Traffic was heavy this morning. Lots of folks heading up the mountain," she commented.

"I don't blame them." Brady O'Ryan, the other paramedic on the crew, refilled his cup. "Everyone wants to make first tracks in the fresh powder."

Bill grabbed a chocolate-frosted doughnut covered with candy sprinkles. "Me, too."

Hansen snickered. "Sucks to be a C shifter."

"I don't see any of you B boys hightailing it out of here to make your mark," Thomas said, with the attitude that had earned her respect at the station.

"Hey, babe." Welton put his arm around the back of her chair. "I'm one of those B boys now."

Her expression softened. "Maybe after we're married, Chief will move you back to Hood Hamlet's elite C squad."

The B boys groaned.

Bill laughed. "Better watch it, guys, or Thomas will dream up yet another physical training torture."

She winked. "Damn straight. And this one will be tougher than the last."

Thomas's last program had nearly killed them all, Bill included. His muscles ached from the memory of the world-class athlete cardio and strength training regimen.

"I've got my skis with me," she told him. "Christian and I are heading up the hill as soon as I'm off. Want to come with us?"

"You're on." But Bill wanted to check on Grace and Liam first. He decided against mentioning them in front of the whole crew. "I'll need to swing by home to grab mine."

"Hey," Welton said. "I heard there was some excitement on your street two nights ago."

"A pickup in a snowbank," Bill said.

Leanne wiped her mouth with a napkin. "Drunk?"

"No, someone trying to make it over the mountain." He didn't want to talk about this now.

"In a blizzard?" Christian shook his head. "Must not be from around here."

Bill stared into his coffee cup. Grace hadn't been stupid. She'd just never driven through the Cascades in winter before. "They're not."

"Injuries?" O'Ryan asked.

Bill eyed what remained in the pink boxes, debating if he wanted another doughnut. "Just sore. They were buckled in. Had air bags."

Thomas raised her cup. "Lucky."

"Very." Though Grace might not agree. Her truck was in bad shape according to Thad. Bill sipped his coffee. "The pickup might be totaled."

"Wonder how they ended up on your street from the highway?" Welton asked. "It's not exactly Main Street."

"No idea." Bill hadn't thought about that. Now he was curious. "I'll have to ask Grace."

Silence fell over the table.

Thomas leaned forward. "Grace?"

Damn. Everyone was looking at him.

"The driver of the pickup." He tried to backtrack slowly, like a truck stuck in a rut. "She showed up at my house needing help."

"Unbelievable." Hansen rolled his eyes, the gesture matching the disdain in his voice. "Even when Paulson can't date a woman, they show up in the middle of the night knocking on his door."

Bill straightened. "It's not like that."

"So she's not hot," O'Ryan said.

He looked up. "I never said that. But she's a mom."

Thomas elbowed him. "Moms can be cute."

"Moms can be hot," O'Ryan said.

Hansen sneered. "Ever hear the term MILF?"

Thomas glared, shutting them all up. "Were Grace's kids in the truck?"

"One kid," Bill answered, knowing how hard car accidents involving kids were for Leanne. Her parents and two brothers had been killed in a crash on Highway 26. She'd been the lone survivor. "He's fine, but had a rough time last night. Kept waking up."

Thomas's forehead wrinkled. "How do you know that?"

Now everyone knew everything. Bill never had been good at keeping secrets. Especially here. He'd had no siblings growing up, but these people were his brothers and sister. Irritating at times, but still family. Though not quite the same as what he'd felt with Grace and Liam.

Bill shrugged. "They're staying at my house."

Looks flew across the room faster than freestylers off the jumps at Timberline's aerial park. Bill sucked it up and waited.

"This woman…" O'Ryan sounded surprisingly earnest. Sometimes he could be a jerk. "She's there now? While you're here?"

Bill nodded. "They were asleep when I left."

Hansen hung his head. "Bad move."

"Why is that?" Bill asked.

Leanne touched his arm. "You don't know them."

"I do now. What would you do? It's a woman and a kid with a wrecked vehicle." He glanced at each of the firefighters. "Which one of you would have done it differently?"

No one. Bill knew that in his heart.

Hansen shook his head. "How can you be such a player and so stupid about women at the same time?"

"She could be trying to get her hooks into you," O'Ryan said. "A mom looking for a sugar daddy for herself and kid."

"I bet a U-Haul truck is at your house now and some sketchy looking dude is loading everything you own to sell on Craigslist," Hansen said.

Bill's jaw tightened. "Grace is not like that."

"You're not at all suspicious?" Thomas asked.

"It's the other way around." He remembered the wariness in Grace's eyes the night she arrived. He was so glad she smiled now. "She called the sheriff on Sunday night. She wasn't sure if it was safe to stay at my house."

Thomas smiled. "Sounds like a smart woman."

"Grace is," Bill said. "She's a widow. Her husband was a Ranger killed in Afghanistan. She's on her way from Columbus, Georgia, to Astoria to make a new start. Or was until she hit the snowbank. Helping her out is the least I can do."

No one said anything for a minute.

Hansen snickered. "At least that's the story she told you."

A series of tones sounded. "Rescue 1 and Engine 3 responding to car accident. Automobile versus pedestrian on the corner of Main Street and Second Avenue," the female dispatcher announced.

Everyone from C shift rose from the table.

Bill headed toward his bunker gear.

O'Ryan followed him. "Way to go, finding a way around no dating in December."

"Huh?"

"Having wild monkey sex with your new roomie, Grace."

Only in Bill's dreams. Though sex would be the easy part. The rest was what he couldn't handle. He removed his shoes and stepped into his bunker pants and boots. "I'm not doing this to get laid. Plus she's got a kid."

"So what?" O'Ryan shrugged on his jacket. "The chick's only passing through town. Sex is sex."

Bill balled his hands, ready to punch the guy. But the clock was ticking. He grabbed his helmet. "How would you know about sex? I thought you were saving yourself for your wedding night."

He climbed into the rig.

Damn O'Ryan. Bill didn't want to be thinking about Grace and sex.

The engine pulled out of the bay, lights flashing and sirens roaring.

This wasn't the time to fantasize. Grace wasn't a woman to lust after, not with appealing and playful images running through his mind and sending his temperature spiraling. He shouldn't be thinking about her romantically at all. He couldn't give her what she needed, what she deserved.

Bill hoped she heard good news about her truck. The sooner she was on her way to Astoria, the better off they all would be.

CHAPTER SIX

THE SOUND OF the garbage disposal woke Grace. Sunlight streamed through the edges of the window blinds.

Morning already?

She didn't want to believe it. Neither did her heavy, let's-go-back-to-sleep eyelids.

The digital clock on the nightstand read 8:26 a.m.

Not early, even if it felt that way.

Grace rolled onto to her side toward Liam. He slept like a hibernating bear. Since he'd been up and down all night, she wasn't surprised.

Too bad she couldn't blame Liam for her exhaustion. Images of the truck and Bill had etched themselves into her mind. A swirling mix of dreams and thoughts had made for a sleepless night. She hoped her and Liam's restlessness hadn't kept Bill awake. He needed his sleep if he was going to be working a twenty-four hour shift.

Another noise sounded—cabinets creaking open and shut.

Bill must be going in late this morning. She could apologize for Liam's behavior.

Grace slid out of bed, careful not to wake Liam. He

would be cranky enough, with Bill at work. She didn't need her son tired, too.

In the hallway, she rolled up the waistband on Bill's pajama pants. Liam had wanted her to wear them again last night. She liked the softness of flannel even if the jammies didn't fit.

She shuffled down the hallway.

A faucet ran.

Weird.

She'd cleaned the kitchen before going to bed last night. Maybe Bill had made himself breakfast. But she didn't smell food. No coffee. And he'd said nothing would keep him from work.

She slowed her pace and lightened her step. If Bill was at work, who was in the kitchen?

She peeked around the corner.

A fiftysomething woman stood at the sink looking down at the running water, a blue sponge in her hand. Her short brown hair was stylishly cut, her makeup perfectly applied. Candy cane earrings dangled from her earlobes. Snowmen covered her red sweater. Not exactly what a cleaning woman would wear. Or a prowler.

Grace waited, watched, grew impatient. She couldn't stand here spying all day. "Hello."

The woman looked up. She gasped.

Grace held up her hands. "I'm sorry if I startled you."

"Who are you?"

"Grace Wilcox." She waited for the woman to offer her name. She didn't. "Bill's, um, guest."

"I'm Mrs. Paulson." Her gaze ran the length of Grace, taking in her messy hair and too big pajamas. "Bill's mother."

The unfriendly tone bristled. Grace overcame the urge to snap back. She needed to be polite. This was Bill's mom. "Nice to meet you. I love your chocolate chip cookies and cocoa mix."

Mrs. Paulson pursed her lips. "You're not the usual type my son brings home."

To sleep with.

The words were unspoken, but implied.

Grace didn't know what to say. Knowing someone for what—thirty-six hours?—didn't make them friends, but after spending yesterday together they weren't strangers. "I'm not…"

"His lover?"

Heat rose up Grace's neck. Her cheeks flamed. "Gosh, no. I'm staying here, but in another bedroom."

Mrs. Paulson's brows arched. "Well, you're creative. I haven't heard that one before."

The accusation in her voice twisted Grace's insides a dozen directions. She shouldn't care what Bill's mother thought of her. Yet standing straight was difficult when all Grace wanted to do was squirm. "It's the truth."

"He doesn't usually have his women stay when he's at work."

His women. His here-for-a-good-time women. Grace wasn't one of them. She raised her chin. "I'm from out of town. I hit a patch of ice and my truck slid into a snowbank, so I ended up on Bill's doorstep."

The words rushed from her mouth like water from

a fire hydrant. Needing to shut up, she clamped her lips together.

"This happened last night?" Mrs. Paulson asked.

Grace rubbed her face. "The night before."

"You're not injured?"

Funny, the woman sounded as if she might care. "No."

Mrs. Paulson's lip curled. "So you spent yesterday here, too."

Grace angled her body toward the doorway, wishing Liam would wake up screaming for her. Anything to escape Mrs. Paulson's demeaning glare and resist the growing itch to tell her off. "Yes."

"Leave his pajamas in the bathroom." The woman's dismissal was clear. "I'll wash them after you go."

Mrs. Paulson was a mama bear; no blaming her for that. She seemed to have no patience for Bill's womanizing. Grace agreed with her there, but needed to take a stand. "I'm not going anywhere."

"But—"

"Big dude…!" Arms outstretched, Liam skidded around the corner in his footie pajamas. One look at Mrs. Paulson had him darting behind Grace quicker than a camera flash.

"It's okay." She reached behind to reassure him. "This is Bill's mom, Mrs. Paulson."

Liam peeked around Grace's hip, then hid again.

A puzzled expression crossed Mrs. Paulson's face. "Who is this?"

"My son. Liam."

An unexpected smile replaced Mrs. Paulson's

scowl. The change was dramatic. She looked ten years younger and ten times nicer. She must like kids better than women wearing her son's jammies. "Hello, Liam."

His little fingers dug into Grace's legs.

She patted his hand, trying to release his death grip on her. "It's okay."

"How old are you, Liam?" Mrs. Paulson asked.

He stuck three fingers out to the side, then added a fourth.

"Three and a half," Grace said.

Liam poked his head out. "Almost four."

"Almost four," Mrs. Paulson repeated. "You're a big boy."

Liam jumped to the left like a jack-in-the-box on its side. "Big and strong like Bill."

"Yes, you are." She studied him, then looked at Grace. "You said you were from out of town."

"Georgia."

"What brings you to Hood Hamlet?"

"Just passing through."

Liam looked around. "Bill? Where's he?"

"At work," Grace said.

Liam's lower lip stuck out. Quivered. "Want Bill. Time to play."

She touched her son's shoulder. "We talked about this last night. Bill's working at the fire station."

Liam stared at the floor as if his world had come to an end.

Grace had to admit she, too, would rather be speaking with Bill than Mrs. Paulson. Damon's mom hadn't liked her much, either. Maybe it was a mother-with-sons thing. Grace vowed not to be like that when Liam brought a girlfriend home someday. "Your son is my son's new best friend."

"I'm not surprised. Bill's a kid at heart. That boy will never grow up. Though I wish he'd find a good woman and settle down." Mrs. Paulson removed a cookie from the cookie jar and gave it to Liam. "This will make you feel better."

Grace sighed. "This is the second day in a row he's had a cookie for breakfast. He'll be spoiled rotten by the time we leave."

"Nothing wrong with a little spoiling," Mrs. Paulson said. "I do that with Bill. I was wondering why the house looked cleaner than usual this morning. You must have dusted and vacuumed. Decorated the tree and the house, too."

The woman didn't sound pleased, but Grace wasn't going to let Bill's mother get to her. She had allowed that to happen with Damon's mom. "The least I could do. I'm so grateful for Bill's hospitality. I plan on doing as much as I can for him in return."

"Thoughtful, but unnecessary. I come over the mornings he works at the station, to help out. He claims I do too much for him, but he gets distracted with his rescue work, climbing and skiing. Someone needs to take care of him."

Grace didn't know what to say. From the time she was twelve she'd done laundry, cleaned the house, washed dishes and cooked meals. Her parents' high expectations had led Grace to work hard around the house and at school to make good grades. As long as she met their demands, everything was fine. If she didn't, they'd made her feel like a stray cat they regretted bringing into the house. "Bill's lucky to have a mother who wants to do so much for him."

Mrs. Paulson focused on Liam, who ate the cookie. "You'll understand when your son gets older. They grow up so fast."

Grow up were the key words here. Grace hoped by the time Liam was thirty he would want to take care of himself, and she would let him.

Mrs. Paulson walked back to the kitchen. "What would you like for breakfast, Liam?"

"Eggs and toast, please," he answered.

The woman beamed brightly. "Such manners."

The surprise in her voice made Grace grit her teeth. "I can make you breakfast, Liam. I'm sure Mrs. Paulson has a lot to do this morning."

"Not as much as I had planned, thanks to you." The words didn't sound like a compliment. "I'm happy to scramble eggs and make toast."

"With jelly." Liam followed the woman into the kitchen, as if being related to Bill automatically made her another friend. "I help."

"I'd love your help. Bill used to help me cook when he was your age." The smile on Mrs. Paulson's face turned genuine. She looked at Grace with appreciation. The woman must be lonely. "Go ahead, take a shower and get dressed. I'll watch Liam."

No way. Bill's mom might be lonely, but Grace wasn't about to leave her son with her. "Thanks, but

Liam isn't used to being around people he doesn't know."

Mrs. Paulson tsked. "Don't you worry. Liam will be fine with me. Won't you?"

"I fine." He opened the refrigerator for her. "Eggs inside here."

With her head in the fridge, Mrs. Paulson waved in Grace's direction. "Go on, now."

Liam mimicked the gesture. "Go, Mommy."

Something about the Paulson family made Liam feel comfortable, in a way he'd never been with anyone but her. Grace, on the other hand, felt nothing but tension, a different kind with Bill than with his mother.

Grace didn't like to be dismissed, especially by her son. Mrs. Paulson approved of Liam, not her. Bill's mother likely thought she was another one of Bill's women du jour. But tense run-ins with Damon's mom had taught Grace not to get huffy. She'd have to earn Mrs. Paulson's respect with charm, no matter how much it irked.

And she shouldn't be complaining.

A shower alone would be great. Her second one in as many days. A record.

"Thank you, Mrs. Paulson," Grace said with a slow Southern smile and sweet drawl she'd learned in Georgia. "I sure do appreciate the help."

The older woman looked startled. "Why, you're welcome, Grace. I promise, Liam will be fine. If he needs you, we'll come get you."

She nodded, then walked down the hall, thinking. She didn't know why she'd tried so hard to end their tense meeting with a draw. She and Liam would likely be gone the next time Bill's mom showed up.

Grace might not understand her behavior, but she knew one thing—no woman would meet Mrs. Paulson's standards for her son.

Thank goodness Bill didn't plan on settling down anytime soon. He would need years to find a wife his mom considered to be a "good woman."

Bill's shift flew by, with not a lot of downtime between calls except for a five-hour stretch of sleep. Now it was Wednesday morning. Time to head out.

He wondered how Grace and Liam had fared alone.

Bill hoped they were doing well, stuck in his house for the past twenty-four hours. He hadn't thought to leave them transportation or his cell number or a key. Most of his houseguests spent the night and were gone the next morning. No one ever stayed longer.

"Paulson." Thomas had changed into ski clothing—insulated pants and soft shell jacket. Two long braids hung from her pink-and-purple fleece cap. She might be "one of the guys," but according to Christian she liked girlie things, too. "See you on the hill."

Bill would swing by home, check on his houseguests, grab his gear and be on his way. "Won't take me long."

Fifteen minutes later, he opened his front door.

Christmas carols played. The scents of cinnamon and vanilla filled the air.

He took another sniff. His mouth watered. Whatever was cooking smelled delicious.

He closed the door behind him.

Liam ran from the kitchen-dining area, his arms outstretched and mouth open. He barreled into Bill, hugging him tight. "Big dude is home."

Warmth pressed down on the center of his chest. No one had ever welcomed him home like this. He lifted Liam into his arms. "How's it going, bud?"

Liam cuddled and rested his head against Bill's shoulder. "Going great now."

A figure-eight-shaped knot formed in Bill's throat. He tightened his grip on the boy, who squeezed back, his little fingers holding on as if Bill was as important to him as his beloved Peanut.

Unexpected warmth flowed through Bill. This was a different feeling than holding a soft, sweet-smelling woman. Different, but good. He didn't want to let go of the kid.

Whoa. What was he thinking? Maybe five hours of sleep last night hadn't been enough. "Where's your elephant?"

Liam squirmed.

Bill placed him on the ground.

The kid ran to the kitchen, darting past Grace, who stood in the doorway. She wore a pair of boot-cut jeans and a baggy forest-green, long-sleeved T-shirt that hid her waistline and chest. The kind of shirt women wore when they didn't want a man to notice their assets.

But Bill already knew.

Grace was luscious. His good manners, not her cam-ouflage shirt, kept her safe from prying eyes and fingers. Though the thought of slipping his hands up her shirt made his mind go blank and his temperature rise.

Stop. He'd gone over this. Seducing Grace would be wrong. She needed someone reliable, someone long-term, someone not destined to repeat the mistakes of his father.

Bill wasn't about to hurt a woman and child with false promises and vows.

"Good morning." She wiped her hands on a dish towel. "Your welcoming committee has been waiting for you. Liam has been up since six."

Bill wished she wanted to be part of the committee, too. He liked being welcomed home. Especially with her wearing those jeans. Unlike her blouse, the denim hugged the curve of her hips nicely, leaving nothing to his imagination. "No sleeping in for you."

"I'm used to it. How was your shift?"

"The same as usual. Whatever you're making smells delicious."

Grace and the aroma of her cooking dragged him in like a tractor beam.

"Baked French toast." She glanced back in the direction Liam had gone. "It's almost ready if you want some."

Bill looked at his watch. He was supposed to be meeting Thomas and Welton to ski, but he didn't want to be rude. He would text Leanne to let her know he was running late. "Sounds great."

"I'll add another place setting to the table."

His table never had place settings. Not until Grace arrived. He liked coming home to food cooking, and sitting at the table together for a meal, something he had only at his parents' house during holidays.

He followed her into the kitchen.

Liam sat on the floor next to the plastic bin full of toys Bill had brought in from the truck. Laughing, the kid held Peanut with one hand and an airplane with the other.

"Settling in," Bill said.

"I hope that's okay."

She sounded nervous. He wanted to reassure her. "It's fine."

And it was. Surprisingly.

He liked coming home not to an empty house, but one full of warmth and laughter and home cooking. This was what Hughes, Porter and Moreno must mean when they talked about their families and wanting to be home. Well, except the cooking for Hughes. His wife, Zoe, could burn water. "I didn't leave you with transportation if you needed groceries or something."

"You're pretty stocked with groceries for a guy who lives alone." Grace motioned to the bag of powdered sugar, the can of whipped cream and what looked like defrosted berries. "We had everything we needed and then some, thanks to your mom."

His stomach plummeted to his feet and kept right on going. "My mom was here?"

"Tuesday morning."

He smacked his forehead with his palm. "I forgot to tell her not to come."

"We were both a little...startled. Your mom thought I was one of your women."

"She didn't."

"She called me your lover."

"I'm sorry." And he was. "My mom has definite views about the women I date. She doesn't approve of any of them. Thinks I can do better."

"At least she loves you."

He still couldn't believe how badly her parents had treated her and Liam. "I'm sorry about your folks. Maybe time has softened their hearts."

"I've tried. I finally gave up. They want nothing to do with us." Grace's voice held no regret, only resignation. "Your mom's a little over the top, but it's nice to see a parent care so much for her child."

"I'm all my mom has."

"Only kid?" Grace asked.

"Yeah. When I was seven, she got pregnant again, but she miscarried and couldn't have any more children."

"That had to have been rough."

He blamed himself. "My dad wasn't here when it happened. Just me. I had no idea my mom was in such bad shape."

"You were only seven. How would you know?"

Bill shrugged.

"Where was your dad?"

"Away. He works in the petroleum industry. When he's not on an oil platform in the Gulf, he's in the Middle East. It's been that way for as long as I remember," Bill said. "If my dad spent more time here in Hood Hamlet, my mom could focus on him, not me."

"Is your dad old enough to retire?"

"Nope. I'm going to have to suck it up until then."

"You're a good son."

He had no choice. At times he appreciated everything his mom did for him. Other times he hated it. But what could he do? She was his mother. "I'm her only son. Any word from the claims adjustor?"

Grace checked the oven and added two minutes to the timer. "I should hear something today. Thad says the body damage is fixable. But the engine isn't."

"The snowbank took out the engine?"

"The motor started sounding funny as soon as we crossed the Georgia state line. But I thought we'd make it."

"What are you going to do?"

"Hear what the adjustor says first. The truck belonged to my husband, so I'd rather not get rid of it."

"Thad's a great mechanic. He'll take care of you and your pickup. I'm happy to do whatever I can."

Gratitude shone in her eyes. "Thanks so much. For everything."

"You're welcome." Bill wasn't quite sure why he said the words. He hadn't done anything. Not really. Giving her a place to stay wasn't costing him anything. Playing with her kid was fun. Spending time with her was no hardship at all.

He wished he could do…more.

He wanted to wipe away the worry from her forehead. He wanted to erase the dark circles below her eyes. He wanted to kiss away the tightness around her mouth. He focused on her full lips. No colored lipstick, shiny gloss or plumper needed.

He wanted to kiss her.

Badly.

His heart rate increased, accelerating like a snare drum roll. His temperature rose twenty degrees as he thought about his lips against hers. His gaze lingered on his target, waiting for a sign, an invitation.

Look away, a voice cautioned.

Bill didn't. He couldn't.

Not when everything inside of him was screaming, *Kiss her!*

Buzz-z-z.

The oven timer blared.

What the hell was he doing? Thinking?

He looked away, stepped back, took a deep breath.

This wasn't only about kissing her. Something about Grace affected him at a much deeper level, in a way no other woman had. She had him thinking about meals together, kids. He didn't like that.

Liam ran to the table. "Breakfast!"

Grace walked to the oven. "Yes, it's time for breakfast."

For them, yes. Not Bill.

She bent over to remove the pan from the oven, giving him a great view of her butt.

Curvy. Sexy.

Damn. Bill rubbed his hand over his chin. He needed to get out of here before he did something he would regret. Something he couldn't take back. "Can you make mine to go?"

Confusion clouded her eyes. "Sure."

Bill didn't blame Grace for the uncertainty in her

voice. He'd said yes to breakfast. He hadn't stopped her from setting the table. But he couldn't forget he wasn't part of the Wilcox family. They weren't part of his. "I'm supposed to go skiing with a friend from the station. I thought I'd have enough time...."

"Not a problem."

Grace used an oven mitt and a hot pad to remove the casserole dish. She placed the baked French toast on the stove.

Oh, man, that looked and smelled like heaven on earth. His stomach rumbled. Nothing like home cooking.

She opened a cabinet. "I saw a plastic container in here somewhere."

He felt like a jerk for bolting on breakfast. "The cabinet on the left."

"Sit, Big Dude." Liam sounded like a little prince with his command. "Eat."

Bill wanted to join the kid at the table. He wanted to spend the day with Liam and Grace, but couldn't give in to temptation.

He'd never experienced this soothing warmth flowing through his veins, this desire to cancel a day skiing and kick around at home. This wasn't about getting naked and doing the horizontal mamba. That he understood. This was...different.

Whatever was going on, sweet as it felt, had to end. Right now.

Bill had everything he needed to be happy—friends, the mountain, powder and a cell phone contact list full of hot women's numbers. No reason to let some kid, his mom and her home cooking change anything.

Bill was going to stick to the way he did things.

He was not going to mess up her life. Or his.

"No can do, bud." Bill went to ruffle the kid's hair, but thought better of it. He pulled his hand back, plastered his arm against his side. "But I'll be home later."

Much later.

After he skied hard, the only thing he'd want to do was fall into bed.

Alone.

CHAPTER SEVEN

EARLY EVENING, BILL entered the Hood Hamlet Brew-pub with Thomas and Welton. Their stomachs and throats demanded payment for a long day skiing. The booths and tables were full, so they snagged three stools at the bar. A perfect way to spend an evening—with beer, burgers and good friends.

Multicolored lights from the garland hanging above them made the glossy wood surface look polka-dotted. Christmas carols played from overhead speakers. OMSAR friends—Sean and Zoe Hughes and Tim and Rita Moreno—were crammed into a booth near the fireplace.

The bartender set three pints on the bar.

Bill raised his beer, stared at the dark ale and creamy foam on top. "Nothing like one of Porter's microbrews after a bluebird day on the mountain."

"You deserve a pint or two after hitting the slopes so hard today." Welton lifted his pint. "Looked like you were trying to outrun an avalanche."

Thomas swiveled toward Bill, staring over the rim of her glass with a pointed look. "Or a woman."

"Don't know what you're talking about." He shifted

on the leather-covered bar stool. His muscles ached from making tracks and carving turns. A good feeling, like when he'd been home this morning.

He shook the thought from his head, the way he'd been doing all day whenever Grace and her son crossed his mind. He shouldn't be thinking about her. She deserved a lot more than a guy like him could give. "Just enjoying the powder."

Thomas faced forward. "Mom alert."

Grace was here? Anticipation surged. Bill straightened, glanced over his shoulder.

His mother was marching toward him with a fiery look in her eyes. The smiling snowman on her sweater emphasized how badly her lips were puckered. He doubted she'd been sucking lemons.

That meant one thing.

Dad had let her down. Again.

Bill tightened his grasp on his glass.

Only his father had that kind of effect on her. Dad must have called to say he wasn't coming home for Christmas. So much for enjoying a little après-ski with his friends. But if his mom put out a distress call, he was the first responder. He couldn't always fix her problems or meet her needs, but he could at least be there for her. Unlike his dad.

Bill gulped the rest of his beer, set the empty glass on the bar, then turned around with his you're-the-best-mom-ever smile. "Hey, Mom. What are you doing here?"

She stood, arms crossed, as if she'd clocked him

going ninety with a radar gun. A corner of her mouth twitched. "Is he yours?"

"Huh?"

"Liam." She took a step closer and lowered her voice. "Is he your son?"

The air whooshed from Bill's lungs. "What in the hell are you talking about?"

"Don't swear."

"Don't provoke me."

Her gaze narrowed. "Liam looks like a younger you. Same coloring. Mannerisms."

"The kid is three. He looks like a lot of people."

Bill is the best daddy.

He'd thought Liam's words were sweet the other day. Now Bill forced himself to breathe, to loosen the tension knotting his insides. And tried not to admit how much he liked hearing those words. He'd be a crappy dad. He didn't have a father to use as a role model. He wouldn't know how to be a good dad.

"He's not mine." Bill kept his voice even, his tone calm. Losing his cool with his mother would only make this worse. "Met the kid and his mom for the first time on Sunday night."

"But—"

"No buts." Rumors spread faster than the norovirus in Hood Hamlet. Though he trusted Thomas and Welton, who were facing the bartender and pretending not to be eavesdropping, but no doubt listening. "Liam's father was an Army Ranger killed in Afghanistan. A true American hero, named Damon Wilcox."

His mother started to speak, then stopped herself. "Grace is a widow?"

Bill nodded.

His mother wrung her hands.

Dread shot down his spine like a snowboard without a leash on a steep, black diamond run. "Please tell me you didn't mention this to Grace."

"I didn't, but... Why didn't you tell me about Grace and Liam?"

Bill rubbed his chin. "Nothing to tell."

"She and her son are staying at your house."

"Temporarily."

"They've been there since Sunday."

"It's only Wednesday."

"So they're leaving soon."

"That's the plan."

"Grace is attractive. Strong. Stands up for herself."

Funny, those were the most positive compliments his mother had ever said about a woman he'd gone out with. Not that he and Grace were dating. He weighed how to best respond. "Yes, but she's not my type."

The truth, but that hadn't stopped him thinking about the way she hummed Christmas carols, and how cute she looked in his pajamas, and the sexy way she filled out her jeans. No worries. He appreciated women. That didn't mean he wanted to go out with all of them.

"I thought your type was female and over the age of eighteen," his mother said.

"Drop it." Bill's words came out sharper than he intended. "Grace and Liam staying with me is no big deal. Her truck's wrecked. She's trying to figure things out. I'm doing what anyone else in town would do for the family of a fallen hero. End of story."

Her mother arched a finely plucked brow. "If you say so."

"I do." His jaw tensed. He didn't want to talk about this any longer. "Anything else?"

"No, except…"

Here we go. He needed a refill. Maybe two. "What?"

"Be careful."

"Don't go all Mama Bear on me." Frustration laced each word. "There's no need for you to worry about me where Grace is concerned."

"I'm not worried about you. Everyone in Hood Hamlet knows you're a big flirt and charmer, with no intention of settling down with one woman." The lines around his mother's mouth deepened. "But Grace doesn't know you or your reputation. Be careful you don't break her heart."

Surprise hit first, followed by a stab of guilt. "You're way off base here."

"Am I?"

"Completely. I don't hit on women with kids."

Never had. Never would.

Even if she was pretty, with a sweet smile, made amazing baked French toast, and showed backbone, struggling to build a life for her and her son. Okay, Bill had flirted a little and convinced her to stay with him, but he refused to follow his standard operating position and take things further. "I admire Grace. She's got…"

"Gumption."

"Yes," he agreed. "I'm not going to put any moves on her."

"Then I guess I have nothing else to say." His mother patted his shoulder. "If you drink too much, call. I'll drive you home."

A noise sounded next to him. Thomas. Laughing under her breath.

Bill fought the urge to roll his eyes. "Thanks for the offer, Mom, but I know my limits."

"I hope so." With that, she left the brewpub.

"Dude." Welton gave Bill a sympathetic look. "The next round's on me."

"This has to go into the annals of Mama Bear Paulson lore." Thomas's laughter spilled out. She wiped the corner of her eye. "I thought she was going to pull out a swab and DNA you right here."

"I can't believe your mom's worried about Grace," Welton said. "Never thought I'd see the day Mrs. Paulson thought angel Bill could do wrong, but all Hood Hamlet, including your mother, knows you're a heartbreaker."

"Shut up." Tonight was looking like a good night to get drunk. But Bill would walk home before calling his mom.

Hansen walked up. "Get enough freshies today?"

O'Ryan stood next to him, looking off into the dining area.

The bartender placed three more pints on the bar.

Nothing beat a Wy'East Brewing Company beer. Except for a free one. Bill reached for his glass. "I can never get enough."

FREE Merchandise is 'in the Cards' for you!

Dear Reader,

We're giving away FREE MERCHANDISE!

Seriously, we'd like to reward you for reading this novel by giving you **FREE MERCHANDISE** worth over **$20**. And no purchase is necessary!

You see the Jack of Hearts sticker above? Paste that sticker in the box on the Free Merchandise Voucher inside. Return the Voucher promptly...and we'll send you valuable Free Merchandise!

Thanks again for reading one of our novels—and enjoy your Free Merchandise with our compliments!

Pam Powers

Pam Powers

P.S. Look inside to see what Free Merchandise is **"in the cards"** for you!

Detach card and mail today. No stamp needed.

FREE MERCHANDISE VOUCHER

2 FREE
BOOKS
and
2 FREE
GIFTS

Please send my Free Merchandise, consisting of
2 Free Books and **2 Free Mystery Gifts**.
I understand that I am under no obligation to buy
anything, as explained on the back of this card.

119/319 HDL F44D

Please Print

FIRST NAME

LAST NAME

ADDRESS

APT.#   CITY

STATE/PROV.   ZIP/POSTAL CODE

NO PURCHASE NECESSARY!

BUSINESS REPLY MAIL
FIRST-CLASS MAIL   PERMIT NO. 717   BUFFALO, NY

POSTAGE WILL BE PAID BY ADDRESSEE

HARLEQUIN READER SERVICE
PO BOX 1867
BUFFALO NY 14240-9952

NO POSTAGE
NECESSARY
IF MAILED
IN THE
UNITED STATES

O'Ryan nudged Hansen. "Who's the hot babe with Thad Humphreys?"

Thomas sighed. "Guys…"

"If you know her, Thomas, you gotta tell me her name," O'Ryan urged. "I think I'm in love."

Hansen snickered. "Lust, dude. Love is for fools."

"You're the fool if you feel that way." Leanne glanced back. "She's pretty, but I've never seen her before."

O'Riley sighed. "Someone has to know who she is."

Hansen looked over. "Her rack could be bigger, but I'd forget about the no dating in December decree for a piece of that action."

Leanne sneered. "Hard to believe you don't have a girlfriend with such sweet talk, Hansen."

Always willing to admire a pretty woman, Bill swung his stool around. He scanned the tables in the back room until his gaze zeroed in on Thad at a table with…Grace and Liam.

Bill's heart slammed against his ribs. He slid from his seat, pushing back the stool until it crashed into the bar. His hands clenched, balling into fists, wanting to punch something, someone. He swore, releasing a tirade about one of the nicest guys in town, even knowing Thad was working on Grace's truck.

"Just a hunch, but I'd say the woman's name is Grace." Leanne dug her fingers into Bill's shoulder, holding him back. "Your eyes are green when they should be blue. Don't fly off like a kamikaze. Sit and cool off for a minute."

Bill didn't get jealous; he simply moved on. The way he felt now was illogical, yet he couldn't help himself.

Hansen's eyes widened. "Isn't Grace the name of the mom who's staying with you?"

He nodded, his stomach churning.

The smiling threesome looked cozy and comfortable, like a family out to dinner and a movie. Thad was single and liked pretty ladies as much as the rest of them. The mechanic's interest in Grace might not be one hundred percent professional. Of course it wasn't. The guy had taken Grace and her son out to eat. This was as close to a date as they came.

"Dibs," O'Ryan called.

"Looks like Thad got dibs in first," Leanne teased.

O'Ryan shrugged. "I'll settle for seconds. She looks sweet. Perfect to kiss under the mistletoe or unwrap on Christmas Eve."

Bill's jaw clenched. Every single muscle bunched. He leveled a death-ray glare at the paramedic. "Don't even think about it."

At the Hood Hamlet Brewpub, Grace squirted ketchup onto Liam's plate. She smiled at Thad, the handsome owner of the body shop. "Thanks for the ride to and from your garage. Stopping for dinner was a great idea. Looks like we were lucky to get a table."

Thad wiped his mouth with a napkin. "The brewpub is a big hangout for tourists and locals, even on weeknights."

Grace wondered if that included Bill. She glanced

around, but didn't see him. "Well, I'm not surprised. The food's great. I love the pretzels and dipping sauce."

"House specialty." Thad leaned closer, a serious gleam in his eyes. "Do you have any more questions about your truck?"

"No, you've been very thorough."

"It won't take long for us to do some research tonight. The claims adjustor will up her lowball offer."

"I appreciate your help."

"Least I can do." Thad smiled at her and Liam, who dipped French fries in the ketchup. "You two didn't have the best introduction to Hood Hamlet."

"People are making up for our troubles." The atmosphere in the pub was friendly, warm and welcoming. "Does everyone in Hood Hamlet go out of their way to help strangers?"

"Not only strangers, but each other."

"It must be nice to live here. I—"

Liam dropped his fry. He reached sideways, toward the empty seat at the table. "Bill. Bill."

Grace looked up.

Bill was striding toward them full of purpose as if he owned not only the brewpub but the town. His jaw was set. His lips narrowed. His gaze was focused on one thing—her.

Grace's heart jumped, followed by a cartwheel and a somersault.

His carelessly styled, ski-tousled hair shifted with each step. His long-sleeved T-shirt stretched across muscular arms and shoulders. His black ski pants emphasized long, strong legs.

Her pulse sped up. Heat rushed through her veins. She reached for her glass of water and drank. Okay, gulped.

Thad cleared his throat, then stood, his posture stiff. He shook Bill's hand. "Care to join us?"

Bill sat in the chair opposite her. He ruffled Liam's hair. "Enjoying dinner, little dude?"

"Yummy." Liam handed him a French fry. "Eat."

Bill did, his watchful gaze on Grace.

She scooted back in her chair, not liking his predatory stare, as if he wanted a taste of her rather than the French fry.

She tucked her hair behind her ears and looked down, critiquing her clothes. Not that she had much beside jeans, track pants and T-shirts to wear. At least what she wore was clean.

Because the way Bill's gaze had locked in on her made her feel desirable. For the first time in years she felt like a whole woman, not the broken widow of a heroic Ranger. The attention gave her a needed boost of confidence in the female department.

"Get a lot of skiing in?" Thad asked.

"One of the best days up there in a while." Bill looked from Grace to Thad. "Showing Grace and Liam the hot spots in town tonight?"

Thad's smile hardened. "It was either that or have them eat dinner alone at your house."

Veins twitched. Lips thinned. Eyes narrowed.

Weird. She thought they were friends. "Thad drove us to his garage so I could speak with the claims adjustor."

"What's the verdict on the truck?" Bill broke from his stare-down to be civil.

The decisions Grace would have to make soon hit with sudden force, like the long, fast-moving freight trains they'd seen driving across the plain states.

Liam handed him another French fry. "The truck is broken, isn't it, Mommy?"

"Yes, it's very broken." She glanced at her plate, and her half-eaten order of halibut and chips. Her appetite had disappeared. "Thad's been explaining my options."

Bill smirked at the mechanic. "Nice of you to go to so much trouble."

"Just trying to help Grace and Liam." Thad's square jaw jutted forward. "Like you giving them a place to stay."

"That's what we do in Hood Hamlet."

"Exactly."

The undercurrent at the table bothered Grace. Both men were great. Thad was sweet, and Bill made her tummy tingle. Without the other, each guy had been pleasant and kind. Together, not so much. She didn't know their history, but recognized the territorial posturing. She'd seen it in Columbus.

Men.

As if one man's hospitality to two strangers was an affront to the other. She didn't get it. Them.

Liam seemed oblivious to what was going on. He sucked on the straw in his chocolate milk, his small hand touching Bill's larger one.

"So how's Muffy?" A French fry dangled from Bill's

fingers. A mischievous smile lit up his face. "I heard the two of you have been dating."

Grace rolled her eyes and took a long sip of her pale ale.

Thad cleared his throat. "We've gone out a few times. Nothing serious. You went out with her, too."

"Once or twice. I'm not dating anyone now."

"Oh, yeah. It's December." Thad emphasized the month. "Some guys would rather let women fend for themselves at the holidays than cough up money to buy them a present. You've always been a fan of leaving women waiting."

Oh, brother. This could take all night. Grace shoved aside her plate, propped an elbow on the table and leaned her head against her hand, forgotten.

The two men stared at each other, as if sizing up a rival or trying to make him back down.

Forget cutting the tension with a knife. They would need an ax or a chainsaw.

The din of the customers around them rose. Their silence increased the pressure at the table.

Time to intervene. She didn't think logic would help, but needed to say something. "A car might be more practical for me than a truck."

Both men startled, then nodded.

Good. She had their attention. "Though I'm attached to the old pickup and I need a way to get our things to Astoria."

"I have a truck," Thad said.

"So do I." Bill put more ketchup on Liam's plate. "I'm happy to drive your things to the coast."

"Same here," Thad said. "I have an aunt in Long Beach. That's across the Columbia River and a little north. I can stay with her."

Bill grimaced. "You can make the drive there and back in a day."

"Unless Grace needs help unpacking."

"Grace has moved a lot. She knows how to unpack."

Thad shrugged, undaunted. "She still might want help."

Bill scooted forward. "I'm happy to help, too."

She made a T with her hands. "Time out, guys. I was just making conversation. I don't know what I'm going to do yet."

The two men kept glancing at each other, as if checking the other's position.

Liam climbed out of his seat and onto Bill's lap.

Thad's nostrils flared.

Grace shot forward with a thrill.

Okay, she was twenty-six, not sixteen, but she'd never had two guys act this way over her. It was... nice. Immature and silly, but flattering.

"Hey." A pretty woman with braided brown hair and warm brown eyes stood next to their table, with a tall, handsome man behind her. "Enjoying yourselves?"

Thad pressed his lips together.

Bill took a French fry off Liam's plate.

Someone needed to be polite. Grace smiled. "The food is delicious. The beer, too."

"I'm Leanne Thomas. This is Christian Welton." The woman extended her arm. "You must be Grace. Paulson—I mean Bill—mentioned you."

She shook the woman's hand. Bill had called Leanne his best friend. "I'm Grace Wilcox. This is my son, Liam."

Liam burrowed his head between Bill's neck and shoulder.

"Sorry to interrupt your dinner, but I wanted to tell Bill our table's ready. Looks like I was just in time—" Leanne motioned to Bill and Thad "—otherwise these two might have had a territorial pissing match right here in the dining room. Jake wouldn't have liked that."

Bill and Thad united to glare at Leanne.

Grace swallowed her laugh and eyed the woman with respect.

"Jake Porter owns the brewpub," Christian said to Grace.

Liam reached across Bill and grabbed a French fry.

"We wouldn't want to upset the owner," Grace said. "Thanks for diffusing the, um, situation."

Christian winked. "We're firefighters. That's what we do."

The iceberg-size diamond engagement ring on Leanne's finger sparkled. Grace remembered what Bill had said. "I hear congratulations are in order."

"Thank you." Eyes twinkling and face beaming, Leanne held her fiancée's hand. "We're getting married on Saturday."

She looked at Christian with such pure love that Grace's heart ached. She missed having that mutual adoration with someone. The squabbling between Bill and Thad might amuse her, but was no substitute. Not even close. "Best wishes for a happy life together."

The server brought the check.

Bill reached out his hand. "I'll take it."

"No, I will." Thad tried to snatch the bill. "You didn't eat."

Bill kept his arm extended. "My treat for you helping Grace."

"I got it, dude. I invited her to dinner," Thad countered.

They fought like boys seeing who got to shoot the new Nerf gun first. A town the size of Hood Hamlet probably didn't have many single women to choose from. Grace must be the new toy the guys wanted to play with. She sighed, then looked at Leanne. "Are they normally like this?"

"No. Not these two." A puzzled expression crossed Leanne's face. She stared at Bill with Liam on his lap. "This behavior is highly unusual."

Grace was ready to go back to Bill's place. She took the black portfolio from the server. "Dinner is my treat."

Both men protested.

"Sorry, boys." Grace scanned the bill for the total and calculated the tip. She'd always been good with numbers. Now she had a degree in accounting. "You snooze, you lose."

Leanne laughed. "You're going to fit in well around here."

"Thanks, but I won't be here long." Grace removed two twenties and a ten from her wallet, then slid the money inside the folder. "Liam and I will be on our way to Astoria soon."

"Too bad." Leanne sounded genuinely disappointed. "But Astoria isn't that far away."

"Less than three hours," Bill said.

"One hundred and fifty miles at the most," Thad said at the same time.

"As I said, not far." Leanne grinned like a bride on a shopping spree in Tiffany's. "Come on, Bill. Time for dinner."

Leanne and Christian walked to an empty table on the far side of the dining area. Bill remained seated.

"Go on," Grace urged him. "We're finished."

Bill didn't move. "You need a ride home."

"I'm driving them back to the house," Thad said.

"I will."

"Liam's car seat is in my truck."

"I know how to install a car seat," Bill said. "The station holds clinics."

Grace put a hand on his shoulder. "Relax, okay? Liam's tired. You haven't eaten. We're going home with Thad."

"No, you're not," Bill said.

"Yes, I am."

Thad shook his head. "I have to drive Grace home so we can put together a counteroffer for the claims adjustor."

"Counteroffer?" Bill asked.

"The claims adjustor wants to total the truck, but gave Grace a lowball offer," Thad explained. "I'm going to help her research what the truck is worth."

"Then get going. I take it you know what will sway the adjustor."

Thad nodded.

Bill stood, then put Liam back in his seat. "Tomorrow, I'll take Grace to look at a replacement."

Thad rose. "I'll put together a list of reliable, safe vehicles. But don't buy anything without me."

"I'm right here, guys," Grace said to no one in particular.

"Paulson," Leanne shouted. "Get your sorry ass over here. I'm hungry."

His gaze locked on Grace. "I'm starving."

Her pulse skittered.

"Dinner won't take long." Bill's gaze raked over her as if she would be dessert. "I'll be home soon."

Liam clapped.

Grace gulped.

Bill's words sounded like a warning.

Yet anticipation zipped from the top of her head to the bottom of her toes. Awareness of the man thrummed through her veins.

If Grace knew what was good for her, she would call it a night before he arrived home.

Or maybe she would put Liam to bed and take her chances.

Dessert might be exactly what she needed.

CHAPTER EIGHT

Turning his truck onto the driveway, Bill hit the garage door opener. No sign of Thad or his pickup.

Good. Bill didn't want to get into a fight.

The garage door lifted.

His headlights lit up the boxes and plastic bins from Grace's pickup. He tightened his grip on the leather-covered steering wheel.

He wasn't proud of his behavior at the brewpub, but seeing Grace with Thad had turned him into a caveman. He had wanted to stomp on any guy who eyed her as O'Ryan did, or took her to dinner, like Thad. Bill had never felt that way about anyone.

Not even Cocoa Marsh, the only woman he'd ever thought about dating more than a few times.

Bill drove into the garage.

He'd been bummed about Cocoa hooking up with her ex-flame, gold medal snowboarder Rex Billings. Until Bill had met a cute snow bunny a week later. What was that girl's name? She'd been blonde and hot enough to make him forget why he'd been attracted to Cocoa in the first place.

He turned off the ignition and removed the keys.

Over dinner, Leanne had called him on his behavior, rather his "childish, territorial chest-puffing." She could be such a hardnose, but he loved her like a sister. Still, he wasn't about to open up to her.

Not after the abuse he'd received at the station over Cocoa, Leanne's former roommate. Discussing Grace was off-limits with everyone.

He'd backtracked during dinner. Shot from the hip, hoping something he said about boys being boys appeased her. Lied his butt off.

What else could he do?

Admit he thought Grace was hot? That he liked spending time with her and her kid? That he wanted them to stay in Hood Hamlet as long as possible?

Nope. Bill couldn't admit any of those things.

Because they weren't true. Not really.

He exited the truck.

Bill was just a little lonely due to no dating in December. He didn't want a girlfriend. He didn't want a relationship. He sure as hell didn't want a ready-made family.

Monogamy and commitment were not in his DNA. He wasn't going to fail like his dad by saying "I do," when the only words out of his mouth should be "I can't."

He opened the door to the laundry room.

Grace was attractive. But she didn't seem like a fling kind of woman. More like an on-bended-knee-proposal kind. A forever kind.

That was why his mom worried he'd break Grace's heart. Leanne had warned him off over dinner. Even

Christian had pointed out Grace had to be stressed, and needed friends with no agenda.

No problem.

Bill would keep his distance. Be her friend, her bud, her pal. He would treat her like Thomas. Okay, maybe he'd be nicer than that.

Inside the house, he shrugged off his jacket and tossed it on the dryer.

He accepted he wasn't the right guy for Grace, but knew Thad Humphreys wasn't, either.

Sure, Thad was an upright, responsible, respectable citizen. No one in Hood Hamlet would disagree.

Bill walked through the dining area to the living room.

The mechanic spent every New Year's Eve giving free rides to drunk drivers and towing their cars home. He'd dropped out of college at age nineteen to take over his family's garage and support his mother and sisters, after his father had a massive coronary and died at the age of forty-two. Thad had made sure Hannah Bishop's cars ran perfectly, maintaining them for free after Nick died and before she'd married Garrett Willingham.

A good man.

But not the one for Grace, and by default, Liam, since the two were a package deal.

Bill's gut told him Thad was wrong for her. Instincts had kept Bill alive and out of trouble all his life. He trusted his instinct to be right now.

He needed to make sure Grace left town with a reliable vehicle and her heart in one piece. Totally possible. Totally his plan.

Giggles sounded from down the hall.

Liam.

Water ran.

The bathtub.

The door to the hall bathroom was closed, but he heard voices, and water splashed.

Taking a shower sounded good. He needed to wash away the smells of the mountain and sweat. A steady stream of icy water would clear his head and put him in the right frame of mind to see Grace.

Ten minutes later, Bill dried off, feeling clean and smelling better. He'd calmed down about Thad, too. Grace was moving to Astoria to make a fresh start. Getting involved with Thad or anyone in Hood Hamlet would be a complication, something she didn't seem to like. Bill didn't like them, either.

He slid into a pair of flannel sleep pants, then reached for a shirt.

The phone rang.

The receiver wasn't in the charger on the nightstand. He tossed the shirt on the bed, jogged out to the living room and answered the phone. "Hello."

"I hope you're not upset with me."

His mother sounded contrite. She should be.

"Not upset." He cradled the phone against his shoulder as he tied the drawstrings at his waistband. "But you shouldn't go off half-cocked about things and people you know nothing about."

"Perhaps it was wishful thinking on my part."

Yeah, right. She'd been upset, not hopeful. But the last thing he needed was her grandma clock to start ticking. "Just so you know… Not. Going. To. Happen."

"Going skiing tomorrow?"

He was grateful she'd changed the subject. "After I take Grace to look at cars."

"Liam will hate car shopping," his mother said.

"We'll bring toys."

Silence filled the line.

"I'll come over and watch him," his mother offered. "That way Grace can concentrate on looking at cars and not worry about Liam."

"I'll ask her."

"I'll be ready in case she says yes and you want to get an early start."

His mother sounded so enthusiastic about babysitting. That wasn't like her. She volunteered in the nursery at church on Sundays, giving her something to do besides hovering over him. "It's my day off. No early starts unless we're talking Alpine climbing," he answered.

"Let me know what time." His mother made her familiar smacking-kiss noise. "Sweet dreams."

He said good-night and disconnected from the call.

A door shut.

Bill turned and saw Grace standing with an odd expression on her face. "Where's Liam?"

"Asleep. Baths do that to him sometimes." She motioned to the phone in his hand. "Need to make a call?"

"I was talking with my mom. She offered to watch Liam tomorrow while we look at cars."

"You don't have to take me out."

"We're going." His wanting to take her had nothing to do with Thad Humphreys. Bill wanted to help Grace. Getting her a safe, reliable vehicle was the first step to her leaving town. He returned the phone to the charger. "We can take Liam with us if you don't want to leave him with my mom."

Grace walked toward him. "I'm sure Liam would rather stay home and play with your mom than have to look at cars for a few hours."

The baggy T-shirt Grace wore didn't hide the bounce of her breasts. Her hips swayed seductively.

His temperature spiked.

The tip of Grace's tongue darted out and dragged across her lower lip.

Damn, she was sexy.

Look, don't touch.

Except looking might get him in trouble tonight. *Pretend she's Leanne or Zoe or Carly or Hannah.* But all he could see was Grace. "I'll, um, let my mom know. Did Thad help you get what you needed?"

"Yes, he did. He was so helpful. A very nice guy."

Helpful. Nice. Bill wanted to choke. But he was going to be good guy, too, and not say a word. For Grace's sake. "Glad it worked out."

Her eyes shone, sparkled, as if full of tiny diamonds. "Tonight at the brewpub, you and Thad were going at each other."

"Men being men. Nothing else."

"That's what Thad said, too."

Bill rocked back on his heels. "Did he say anything else?"

She closed the distance between them. "Just that he was happy to help me however he could."

"I'm happy to do the same."

"I appreciate that." Something flickered in Grace's eyes. She touched his shoulder.

Her fingertips seared his skin. He sucked in a breath. "What…?"

"You have tattoos."

Heat emanated from the point of contact. His pulse kicked up a notch. Okay, three. "A couple."

"Who's Nick?"

Bill tried to think. Not easy to do with her so close, touching him. He took a deep breath. Focused.

Oh, yeah. The memorial tattoo.

"Nick was a good friend killed climbing Mount Hood." Warmth flooded Bill. He tried not to think about Grace's fingertips outlining the scrolled name. "We grew up together. Hung out. He taught me to climb, fish, hunt. Pretty much everything having to do with the outdoors. He was a couple of years older. The closest thing to a big brother Leanne and I had. Nick was a total jokester, too. He wore the stupidest Santa hat. The ball lit up and turned different colors. We used to give him so much crap over that hat."

"Sounds like a good guy."

"The best. I think about him every day."

Grace trailed her finger down Bill's arm, making his nerve endings dance and spark. "This tattoo looks job related."

"A helmet with our squad name." He ground out the words. If she didn't stop touching him, he was going to want to touch her. He needed another cold shower or a whopping dose of reality. "Did your, um, husband have any tattoos?"

Her lips parted. She pressed her arm against her side. Her hands balled, then she released them.

A mix of regret and relief washed over Bill. He missed her touch, but knew this was for the best—the best for Grace.

She raised her hand and brushed his right biceps, her fingers soft and warm.

Damn, he hadn't expected her to touch him again, but he liked it. More than he should.

"Damon had several." She drew an arc across Bill's skin, sending pleasurable sensations bursting from his nerve endings. "A Ranger Scroll from the 3/75 here."

"Three seventy-five?"

"Third battalion." She traced a line to the back of Bill's shoulders, starting sparks shooting down his arm. "He had the Ranger DUI here."

Bill had no idea what was going on. He didn't care, even if he should. He'd given her the chance to stop. She was the one who started it. Both times. Talk about a turn-on. "I have a feeling that doesn't mean driving under the influence."

"Distinctive Unit Insignia." She drew something on his shoulder blade, making his temperature shoot up another ten degrees. "It's the insignia on a Ranger's tan beret, a shield with four quadrants. One with a sun, another a star and two with a lightning bolt."

Her hand remained on Bill.

His heart pounded, so loud he was aware of each beat. Blood rushed where he didn't want it to go.

Common sense told him to back away. Too bad he

was never one to do what he was told when a beautiful woman was touching him.

Might as well go all in. "Did your husband have any others?"

She ran her fingertip up across Bill's right shoulder to the left side of his chest.

Something fluttered, a tightness, a pang.

"One was right here." She drew a heart. "For me."

His groin tightened. His temperature spiraled until he was downright feverish. All he could think about was kissing her hard on the lips until neither of them could breathe or see straight.

But he couldn't, could he?

Bill tried to focus. He attempted to shut off the X-rated fantasies playing in his mind. All the words of caution from his mom, Thomas and Welton, along with his own, echoed in his brain. He couldn't offer what Grace wanted or needed. Yet here they were....

His gaze locked on hers. "What are you doing?"

She lifted her chin, giving him a great view of her neck, a neck that should be showered with kisses. His kisses.

Her face flushed. "I...I don't know."

That made two of them. "If you don't stop, I'm going to kiss you."

The corners of her mouth curved into a slow smile. "Not if I kiss you first."

Oh, my. Oh, my. Oh, my.

Grace couldn't believe she'd said the words aloud. Oh, she'd been thinking them. Insane.

She forced herself to breathe. Not an easy task when each breath was coming quicker and quicker.

A come-here-sexy-lady grin crinkled the corners of Bill's eyes. "I'm waiting."

Oh, boy. She had never been flirty or forward. Not ever. But seeing Bill shirtless had ignited a fire deep inside her belly. Her fingers had tingled, aching to touch him. She'd wanted two servings of dessert.

Temporary insanity?

More likely loneliness and raging hormones.

But she couldn't help herself.

Memories had stirred. Feelings. Desire.

She'd needed to touch him. So she had.

And now...

Grace stared at his wide shoulders and muscular arms. Her gaze lowered to his solid chest and rock-hard abs. The waistband of his pajama pants rode low on his hips.

She looked up at his face. His mouth. Lips.

One kiss. That was all she wanted. A little kiss.

Something to remember him by. Something secret. Something hers alone.

Grace rose up on her tiptoes. She brushed her lips against his.

Sparks erupted. Heat flared.

Wowza. Forget fireworks. They could have their own Fourth of July celebration right here in December.

She pressed harder against his mouth, soaking up his heat and taste. Her nerve endings shivered. She wanted more.

"Grace…" It sounded like a half groan, half plea. "We shouldn't."

His words proved Bill was a good guy. But she didn't want to stop. "Please. A little more."

There. She wasn't being greedy.

Bill answered her with more kisses. His lips parted, moved skillfully over hers. Tasting, teasing, pleasing.

Grace's legs wobbled, her knees weak from the sensations shooting straight to her toes. Light-headed from the kisses, she leaned against his firm chest.

So strong.

His arms wrapped around her, embracing her with strength and warmth and a sense of belonging she'd never thought she'd feel again.

Stop, a little voice cautioned.

She knew she should.

Everything she was feeling and thinking was telling her to stop.

But she didn't want to stop.

Grace didn't know if she'd ever be kissed this way again. She wanted to make the most of it while she could.

Tongues tangled and danced.

She ran her hands over the muscular ridges of his back and through his damp hair. She couldn't get enough of Bill's kisses, of him.

She was…home.

Panic ripped through her.

Not home. A temporary place. In temporary arms.

He cupped her bottom, pulling her even closer.

She went eagerly, pressing against him. She arched—

"Mommy?"

Grace jumped back as if she'd been shocked by ten thousand volts.

She turned to see Liam, his hair sticking up. He stood in the hallway, holding Peanut against his heart.

Oh, no. She covered her bruised and throbbing lips with her hands. Tried to calm her breathing, cool the heat in her cheeks, pull down the bottom of her shirt.

Bill, his breathing as ragged as hers, walked over to her son and knelt. "What's up, little dude?"

Liam stared at the ground. "Peanut woke up. Mommy wasn't there."

Bill touched the stuffed animal. "As you can see, Peanut, your mommy's right here."

Liam nodded.

Grace pulled herself together and joined them. Kneeling in turn, she touched his shoulder. "Did you wonder where I was?"

Another nod.

She hugged him. "I'm sorry I wasn't there beside you, but it wasn't my bedtime yet."

Liam wrapped his arms around her neck. "Sleep. Sleep."

The last thing she wanted to do was sleep. That meant she should go to bed. "We can sleep now."

She was a mom—Liam's mom. Her son needed her and she needed him. Even if her lips wanted more kisses.

More kisses weren't a smart idea.

The hunger in Bill's eyes matched the way she felt inside. Thank goodness Liam had woken up, or things might have gone further than she intended. "I need to get him to bed."

"I know." Bill brushed his hand over Liam's hair. "Sleep tight, bud."

The little boy's thumb was in his mouth. His eyelids drooped.

Bill cupped Grace's face. "We'll talk about this later."

She'd tried hard to set a good example for Liam, but tonight…

Heat spread up her neck. She couldn't believe her son had caught her making out with the big dude.

Grace stood, then carried Liam to the guest bedroom. She glanced back at Bill. "Let's forget it ever happened."

"I won't be forgetting anytime soon."

Neither would she. But she would have to try.

The bedroom door was open. She stepped inside the room. "Good night."

Bill stood in the doorway. "Sweet dreams."

His gaze, full of desire, made her shiver with want.

Darn the man. She'd likely be having hot dreams because of his toe-curling kisses. "See you in the morning."

"I'll be seeing you sooner." He winked. "In my dreams."

Her mouth dropped open. She stood with her son in her arms, her heart roaring in her ears.

Wicked laughter lit his eyes. Bill twisted the lock on her side of the knob. "Good night, Liam. Gracie."

He closed the door. The latched clicked.

Gracie? No one called her Gracie. Oh, they'd tried.

Damon had given up and called her babe. She'd been named Grace and that was what she wanted to hear.

But the name didn't sound so bad coming from Bill's lips.

She laid Liam and Peanut on the bed and covered them with the sheet and comforter. Her son was sound asleep in a minute.

Grace changed into an Iowa Hawkeyes nightshirt.

Bill Paulson spelled ten types of trouble. He might be a good guy, but his kisses had Bad Boy scribbled all over them. Fun for a moment, dangerous for any longer.

She was clever enough to know better than to mess around with a man like him.

But clever or not, she wanted to kiss the bad boy again. And again. And again.

What was she going to do?

It'll be okay, babe.

"Quiet."

Usually, she welcomed Damon's words and the assurance they promised, but not tonight.

Not when her lips throbbed, not when her heart ached, not when she wanted to fall asleep in another man's arms.

Not any man's. Bill's.

Grace covered Liam with another blanket. He didn't stir.

She would brush her teeth, floss, wash her face, then crawl under the covers to hide. She might not be able to forget the kisses she'd shared with Bill, but maybe she could pretend those kisses had never happened, that she imagined or dreamed them.

That would allow her to sleep.

And she needed sleep. Almost as much as she'd needed kisses.

Bill leaned against the wall next to the guest bedroom door. He didn't know how long he'd been standing in the hallway. He didn't care.

He couldn't remember how many women he'd dated, how many women he'd kissed. But not one had made him want all of her—mind, body and soul—like Grace Wilcox.

He'd felt like a randy teen kissing her, almost losing control, falling over the edge and embarrassing both of them. Well, him.

That had never happened before.

Not even the first time making out with Maggie Freeman in the storeroom of her father's general store on Main Street.

Thanks to Grace, Bill ached with need. He wanted to touch her again, hold her again, taste her again. He shouldn't feel that way about any woman, especially one with a kid. He was too much like his dad to be a forever type family guy. But when she'd touched him, he'd gone mad with desire. When she'd kissed him, he'd struggled to remain in control. When she'd kept kissing him, he hadn't wanted to stop.

The guest bedroom door opened.

Crap. Bill straightened.

Grace stepped into the hallway. Her long brown hair

was messy and tangled, as if she'd changed quickly. A baggy nightshirt hid delicious curves, but the knee-length hem gave him a great view of her calves.

Toned muscle. Smooth, pale skin.

Sexy.

What the hell was wrong with him? He was getting turned on looking at her lower legs.

They were great calves, though.

She left the door ajar.

"Forget something?" He tried sounding casual, as if he hadn't been skulking outside her door, fantasizing.

Grace drew back. Her brow furrowed. "What are you doing here?"

"Thinking about you."

She started to speak, then pressed her lips together. Her gaze bounced from Bill to the guest bedroom door. "I don't have time for this. I need to get back to Liam."

She hurried past Bill, like a gust of wind roaring through the Columbia Gorge. Only this squall swirled around him with a sweet aroma of jasmine and vanilla.

The bathroom door closed. Locked.

Bill fought disappointment and rising frustration. He should have said something different, something more. But retreating wasn't an option. He needed to figure out what was going on.

Maybe he'd misjudged the impact of her kisses. Blown them out of proportion. He hadn't kissed a woman in over a week. He could be imaging things to be better than they were. That would explain his over-the-top reaction.

Bill needed to get her and her kisses out of his system. He knew exactly how to do that.

Kiss her again.

One more kiss would disprove this nonsense. Another kiss would be nice. Special, even. But not enough to change his world—his perfect world.

Kissing her again was a good plan. If Grace agreed…

Minutes ticked by.

Bill waited. He wasn't the kind of guy to swan dive into a foot of water over some woman, let alone a kiss.

All Hood Hamlet, including your mom, knows you're a heartbreaker.

Welton's words echoed in Bill's head. He'd worn the title of heartbreaker like a badge of honor, stepping into the role after Jake Porter and Sean Hughes married. Being called a player brought a rush of pride. Everyone knew, everyone expected that kind of behavior from him.

Everyone but Grace.

Bill didn't want her to find out about his reputation. She didn't seem the type to be impressed by his womanizing, even though he got involved only with women who understood the rules and how he felt about relationships. But Grace might not absolve him of responsibility for any resulting broken hearts.

Not that she had anything to worry about. He would be careful and keep her safe.

But he needed to know if her kisses really made him feel so incredible, so invincible. Or if the December dating hiatus made him kiss-hungry for any pretty woman.

Testing his hypothesis, as his friend volcanologist Sarah Purcell would say, made sense. Another kiss—a test one—wouldn't take long.

The door to the bathroom opened.

His pulse jolted like a Thoroughbred out of the starting gate. But he was feeling like the long shot in the race.

Standing in the doorway, Grace sucked in a breath. "You're still here."

"I want to talk." Not exactly true, but saying "I want to kiss" might freak her out.

"Liam might wake up." She glanced at the bedroom door. "I should get in there."

She should, but Bill didn't want her to go. Not yet. "It won't take long."

The bridge of Grace's nose crinkled, matching the creases on her forehead. She crossed her arms over her chest. "What?"

Truth time. "I want to finish what we started."

She wet her lips. Her eyes darkened, but he couldn't tell if that was due to annoyance or desire. "Here?"

Bill nodded, itching to reach for her.

She looked down at the hardwood floor. "I don't think that's a good idea."

"It's a great idea." Her pulse point, visible at the V of her neckline, beat rapidly. So she wasn't so immune to the charged air between them. Anticipation made him smile. "Think of it as a test. Kissing again will allow us to see it's no big deal."

"You thought it was a big deal?"

"I'm not sure what to think right now."

"That makes two of us. But you shouldn't kiss me again."

"No more kissing?" Bill leaned closer, near enough that she could feel his warm breath against her. "In case you forgot, Gracie, you kissed me."

She flushed. "True, but you kissed me back."

"A gentleman always kisses back."

"That's why you did it? You were being polite?"

His words had hit a nerve with her.

"I'm joking." He raised her chin with his fingertips. "I had to kiss you because were standing under mistletoe."

Grace glanced back at the living room. "There's no… You think this is funny."

"It is funny. You're funny." He let go of her face. "After we kiss, we'll know. We can have a good laugh about all this and move on."

"I have a feeling I'm being led into a trap."

"Never."

Indecision and doubt filled her eyes. "One kiss."

Excitement built in Bill's chest. "One is all I'm asking for."

He lowered his mouth to hers.

Their lips met, soft as a whisper at dawn.

A spark jolted through him. Forget a faint sound, this kiss was an in-your-face, ear-shattering shout.

Exactly like before.

Tingles erupted. Blood boiled. Sensations pulsed through him.

Even more than their first kiss.

She tasted like peppermint, her toothpaste. And warm, like her caring, giving heart.

He was the one caught in a trap, snared by Grace's kiss. He wanted to keep kissing her, but he would keep his word. He'd said one. That was all he would take.

At least tonight.

Bill slowly, regretfully drew it to an end. Not a fluke. He hasn't been imagining things. He hadn't blown anything out of proportion.

Grace's kisses were different. Better. Sexier. Hotter. And the reason he'd been struggling to think straight. "Thanks."

"Satisfied?"

"Very," he admitted. "I figured out what I needed to know."

"Me, too." Without meeting his eyes, she slipped into the bedroom and closed the door behind her.

"Good night, Gracie."

He touched his lips.

One more kiss was not going to be enough.

Bill knew that without an ounce of uncertainty.

Kisses like this didn't happen every day. They would be fools to waste her time stuck in Hood Hamlet.

All he had to do was convince Grace they could be together without him breaking her heart. He would be careful not to hurt her. He *couldn't* hurt her. But the longing in her eyes, on her lips, told him she needed kisses as much as he did.

Maybe even more.

CHAPTER NINE

THE NEXT AFTERNOON, Grace walked along Hood Hamlet's wooden sidewalk with Bill. Christmas lights twinkled in store windows. Snippets of carols drifted out of shops with the opening and closing of doors. Snow fell from the darkening skies, matching the storm brewing inside her.

She stole a sideways glance at Bill, taking in his wool beanie, red plaid parka, gray cargo pants and boots. So handsome, all rugged and outdoorsy and male. She wished she wouldn't notice how he dressed. She wished she could stop thinking about kissing him.

Bill was obviously over their kisses. He hadn't mentioned a word about last night as they'd driven down the mountain this morning and checked out vehicles in the towns of Gresham and Sandy. He hadn't brought up the kisses while sharing a pepperoni-and-mushroom pizza at a small Italian café on their way back up the mountain.

The kisses must have scored "no big deal" on his test.

She would have given them an A+. She'd been up half the night reliving every moment and wanting more.

Grace adjusted the scarf around her neck for the third time in ten minutes. Time to move on. She needed to stop tying herself in knots about what happened last night. She should be happy Bill was taking time on his day off to look at cars and show her Hood Hamlet. Not many people would do that. At least not for her.

Two teenage boys strutted toward them, a swagger to their steps and snowboards resting on their shoulders. The words Hood Hamlet Snowboarding Academy were embroidered on their jackets.

"Those dudes aren't going to get out of our way." Bill slipped his arm around Grace's waist, then pulled her toward a coffee shop. "Wouldn't want you to get knocked down."

Too late. Kissing him had knocked her flat on her face. His touch threatened to do the same thing.

Grace wore a camisole and sweater under her, well, Bill's jacket. In spite of three layers of clothing, tingles and warmth made her all too aware of his hand on her. Of course, having his muscular body against her and his hot breath on her neck weren't helping.

The way he protected her, putting himself between her and the teenagers, sent her pulse sprinting. She'd been taking care of herself for so long, she'd forgotten how nice it was not to have to do everything. Bill made her feel special, treasured.

The snowboarders passed, dropping four letter words like confetti.

"Dudes," Bill called to the boys. "Remember your manners. Doubt you want Johnny to know you're prowling Main Street like a couple of gangstas."

The teens nodded sheepishly. Apologized. Ran.

Grace watched them disappear around the corner, trying to compose herself. "Whoever Johnny is must instill great fear in those kids."

Bill edged away from her. "A little fear, but Johnny Gearhart aims for respect. He's a former snowboarding champion and runs the school."

She fell into step with Bill, ignoring the urge to take his hand. That was what she would have done walking next to Damon. Funny and disconcerting that she wanted to do the same thing now.

"So what do you think of Hood Hamlet?"

"Charming." The Alpine village defined the word, especially with the buildings and streets decked out for the holidays. Garlands and lights draped the storefronts. Wreaths hung on windows and doors. The old-fashioned streetlamps were wrapped in red and white strips like candy canes. "The town looks like a Christmas card."

"It does, but Hood Hamlet's beautiful no matter what time of year." He glanced around with a satisfied look on his face. "I wouldn't want to live anywhere else."

"I can see why." She watched a man dart across the road to pick up a dropped package for a woman juggling shopping bags. "The people seem nice, too."

"We have a few grumpy old-timers who yell at kids. A Scrooge or two who like to hear themselves say 'Bah-humbug' every December, and some teens who make trouble, but the majority are hardworking, good-natured folks."

Two men in a snowboard shop waved to a woman on the sidewalk outside.

Grace had been to Main Street twice. Each time this quaint town called to her—to her heart—like no other place she'd lived. "I wonder if Astoria's like this."

"Astoria is bigger, but you'll find friendly people. You might have to look harder."

She stopped in front of a window display with a "hill" made of white cottony fabric and an old-fashioned toboggan. "Probably won't find much snow there."

No snowmen or snowball fights or snow angels. She sighed, already missing Hood Hamlet.

Bill shot her a sideways glance. "Thinking you might want to stick around town awhile?"

Heat flamed in her cheeks. She wasn't one to long for what she couldn't have. She continued along the sidewalk. "Just making conversation."

"That's what you were doing last night."

He meant at the brewpub, but she couldn't stop thinking about the feel of his skin, the touch of his hands, the taste of his lips.

Do. Not. Go. There.

She cleared her dry throat. "Liam's never had a white Christmas."

"He needs to have one. Spend Christmas in Hood Hamlet."

Her gaze jerked to him. "I wasn't fishing for an invitation."

"I know, but I'm inviting you. Experience Hood Hamlet at its finest. You might see Christmas magic in action."

She let his words sink in. Appealing, yes. Practical, no. "But the twenty-fifth…"

"Is only a week away."

Snow was the reason she was stuck in Hood Hamlet, though the truck's engine might have given out, anyway. The thought of a white Christmas was enticing. This town might not be magical, but it was darn close to a TV Christmas movie setting. The memories made here would last forever. But that would mean more time being tempted by Bill and his kisses. Talk about dangerous. "I…"

"Do you have a place to stay in Astoria?"

Her stomach tensed. "No, but there are temporary rentals available."

"What about a job?"

"No. But thanks to Damon's life insurance and monthly survivor benefit checks, I don't need one right away. I have a degree in accounting and plan on looking for a part-time position once we're settled. Maybe find something during the tax season."

Too long an explanation when a no would have sufficed, but being around Bill made her nervous. She rattled on like a forgotten kettle.

He waved to someone driving by in a blue pickup. "Know anybody in Astoria?"

This one was simple to answer. "No."

"Then why do you need to be there for Christmas?"

Grace didn't. Bill skillfully had her cornered. If she and her son stayed here, Liam could play in the snow after opening his presents. They would be celebrating the holiday in a house with a fireplace to hang stockings on Christmas Eve. She could explain to Liam how Santa came down the chimney. All positives, except... "I don't want to overstay our welcome."

"It's not like you'll be here forever."

No, but forever didn't sound so bad.

She shook some sense into herself.

Forever was as much a fantasy as Christmas magic.

"Stay until the twenty-sixth," he suggested.

"The twenty-sixth?"

"That would give you twelve days in Hood Hamlet. Perfect amount of time, given the holiday season."

She wouldn't go that far. Having an end date made her feel better, but something remained unspoken. The elephant in the room, but its name wasn't Peanut. "What about, um, last night?"

"You mean us kissing?"

She glanced around. "Shhh. Someone might hear you."

"Kissing isn't against the law."

"I felt like I was breaking a few laws."

He eyed her with interest. "Oh, really."

Darn. She hadn't meant to say the words aloud. "Isn't that a pretty wreath hanging on the candy shop?"

"Don't change the subject." He pulled her into an alcove next to the hardware store. "I want you to stay in Hood Hamlet for two reasons. The first is your son. He needs a white Christmas. The second is I want to spend more time with you. There's something between us."

Her heart bumped. Then reality set in. "When we kiss?"

"You felt it, too."

"I did."

"Let's explore the chemistry and enjoy each other while you're in town."

He made being strictly physical sound so easy. But the thought of getting closer terrified her. "What happens when it's over?"

"You go to Astoria like you planned. Until then we'll have fun."

Fun. She had a feeling they had different definitions of the word.

"I don't—" she lowered her voice "—sleep around. I've only been with…"

"Your husband."

She nodded.

"I respect that. I respect you." Bill gazed into her eyes, placed his arms on either side of her with his palms against the wall. "Most people underestimate me, but I'm a man of my word. I won't ask you to do something you're not ready for or don't want. But I'm not going to lie. Kissing you was one of the highlights of my year. And it's been a very good year. I'd like to indulge in a few more kisses, if you're game."

She was. But she'd never approached kissing so casually before. Not with Damon. Not with Kyle. "What if I want to stay for Christmas, but I'm not sure about… us?"

The word *us* sounded funny coming from her lips.

"I want you and Liam to stay no matter what you decide about you and me. Don't answer right now. Think about it."

Grace had a feeling all she would be doing was thinking about it. Imagining it. Craving it. "I will. Thanks."

"Come on. I want to show you something." Bill grabbed her hand and pulled her forward. "Welton Wines & Chocolates is up ahead."

The change of topic brought welcome relief. "The name sounds delicious."

"Christian makes the wines. His cousin Owen is a chocolatier."

"Sounds like two people you want to have as friends."

"Want to go in?" Bill asked.

That sounded better than debating his offer. "I'd rather not miss out on two of my favorite things. But first we should see if your mother minds staying with Liam a little longer."

"No worries. She sent me a text saying not to come home. They're decorating sugar cookies."

Grace's throat clogged with emotion. Her parents had returned his birth notice, unread. Damon's parents had chosen not to be a part of Liam's life. Anger, then grief, had severed the ties completely. Her son had never decorated Christmas cookies with a doting grandmother, had no idea what that would be like. Not until today. The Paulson family's kindness overwhelmed Grace. "I don't want to take advantage of your mom."

"My mom's loving this," Bill said. "She gets lonely, especially when I'm not around. I call and text when I'm working, or if I'm not planning to see her."

"Thoughtful of you."

"I'd like to think so, but she's not happy with me. Chewed me out the other night in the brewpub."

"Why?"

"My mom has strong opinions about my behavior. Especially with women."

"I'm sure that can be a pain, but there are worse things. My parents only cared about me when I did what they wanted."

Bill gave the boardwalk a scuffing kick. "I still can't believe they won't see you."

Resignation fought with loss. She shrugged.

He huffed out a grunt that sounded like "their loss." Then he smiled, making her feel warmer inside. "After hearing about your parents, I shouldn't complain about my dad. He's great at what he does, which is why he's in such high demand far away from us. It's like having a part-time dad. There but kind of not."

Grace nodded. "Sometimes you just have to look at what you have, not what you lost. If you're like your dad in any way, he must be an okay guy. And your mom…she wants to do whatever she can for you. You're lucky to have so many people who love you."

Bill was quiet, his head bobbing slightly, before he looked at her thoughtfully. "You're a kind woman, Grace. My dad will like you. I hope he makes it home for Christmas this year so you can meet him. And I appreciate what my mom does. I am lucky, but I wish she had others to mother hen."

"Your mom likes being with Liam. Maybe you could find other kids for her to spend time with and help."

"Great idea." Bill opened the door. A bell jingled. A smile spread across his face. "Liam would like this place."

"He'd like the bell." The aromas of chocolate and wine filled the air. "And the chocolate."

Bill's eyes twinkled, like Santa here to make her Christmas wishes come true. "What do you like?"

You. Strike that. "Dark and red."

"Bill, Grace." Leanne waved from a back table where she sat with two women. "Come join us."

Grace followed Bill past the display of handmade chocolates on one side and a wine bar on the other to an area of café tables.

Leanne rose. "Grace Wilcox, I want you to meet Zoe Hughes and Carly Porter. Two of my closest friends."

"Nice to meet you." Zoe Hughes was a beautiful woman with long, shiny brown hair, designer clothes and a large baby bump. "I'd stand, but my back has been killing me all day. I think this kid will be our first and last. Hard to believe I still have more than three months to go before this little one arrives."

Grace smiled. "I remember that feeling. Enjoy the peace and quiet while you can."

Carly nodded, her blond ponytail bouncing. A stylish and very pretty woman, she wore a purple sweater with a colorful scarf artfully tied. "Maybe when they go to college it'll happen again."

"Let's not go there." Zoe touched her round belly. "I can't even imagine the terrible twos."

"Don't," Grace and Carly said at the same time.

Leanne shivered. "I'll stick to babysitting."

Grace noticed they were gift wrapping rectangular boxes in red foil paper, white satin ribbon and a sprig of holly. "Getting ready for the holidays?"

"My wedding," Leanne said. "My friend Sarah came up with the idea for these favor boxes. I thought I had everything finished, until she asked me to send her a pic of them wrapped."

"So we're wrapping," Carly said.

Zoe held up a roll of ribbon. "And decorating."

Leanne looked at Bill. "We could use help."

He shook his head. "I'm all thumbs when it comes to gift wrapping."

Grace recalled the present under his Christmas tree, a total mess of crinkled paper and too much tape. "This I can confirm."

Everyone looked at her.

She bit her lip. "I, um, have seen his efforts."

"She's right," Bill agreed. "I suck at wrapping."

"We'll give you a pass this time." Leanne studied him. "I thought you'd be skiing, even though it's probably a whiteout up there by now."

He shrugged. "Had a few things to do."

She raised a brow. "Your mom does everything for you."

The woman's tone made Bill sound like a mama's boy. Grace felt a strong urge to come to his defense. "Bill took me to look at cars and trucks. Mine's in the garage."

The three women exchanged curious glances.

Uh-oh. Grace had the feeling she'd shared too much.

Leanne waved her hand. "Make yourself useful, Paulson. Help Owen load the cases of wine for the reception."

"Aye, aye, Captain." He gave a mock salute. "I trust you'll entertain Grace."

"Hell, no," Leanne said. "I'm going to put her to work."

Honored to be included, she sat. "I'm happy to help."

"Be back soon." Bill walked toward the back of the shop.

Picking up a pair of scissors and a roll of wrapping paper, Grace felt his attention on her. She looked up.

He was glancing back over his shoulder. "Send someone to get me if you need anything."

She nodded.

"So you're staying with Bill?" Carly asked.

"Yes." Grace cut wrapping paper to fit the favor box. "He's been so kind. The answer to our prayers."

A strange tension settled over the table, different from last night.

Zoe looked at Leanne, then back at Carly. "Bill's a great guy."

"He'd do anything to help anybody," Carly agreed.

"True, but let's cut to the chase. You're new in town so we thought you should know." Leanne gave Grace a sympathetic look. "Bill's a player."

Grace cut wrapping paper off one end of the box. She clutched the scissors too hard and the foil ripped. "I know."

The other women looked at her with confused expressions.

"How do you know?" Leanne asked.

Grace didn't understand why Bill's friends were

warning her about him, as if she was blind. Part of her was offended.

But another part appreciated their concern. She'd left behind a network of support at Fort Benning, aka the Wives Club. She taped the wrapping paper. "Bill told me he's happy being single and doesn't plan on settling down anytime soon. His mom said something about the number of women he brings home. I've always been good at math. It wasn't difficult to add things together."

"That's good you figured it out." Leanne rubbed her face. "Bill's great with women. Just look at how well he treats his mom."

Carly leaned toward Grace. "He's a total catch. That's part of the problem. Women want him."

Zoe nodded. "But he backs off before any real commitment can happen."

"He backs off before they're dressed," Leanne said.

Grace tied a white ribbon around the wrapped present, then she pulled the ends so tight the holly's stem bent.

She reminded herself she shouldn't be angry. These women were trying to help her, protect her heart, even if their methods were too blunt. "Just so you know, Bill has been a complete gentleman. When he had to examine me for injuries, he made me feel safe by making sure I knew exactly what he was doing. He treats my son like a little prince."

Carly creased the ends of the wrapping paper. "Bill's always been a sweetheart."

"Except for the incident with Thad at the brewpub, I couldn't ask for a more gracious host." Grace tore off a piece of tape and handed it to Carly. "He invited me to spend Christmas in Hood Hamlet."

"Nothing beats this town for the holidays," Zoe said. "My family is flying in to celebrate with us."

Leanne's gaze didn't soften as expected. Her milk-chocolate eyes darkened to the color of 86% cacao. "Have you agreed to spend Christmas here, Grace?"

"Yes, I have."

Leanne tugged on one of her braids, her lips pressed tightly together.

That was when Grace knew. This was as much about protecting Bill's heart as hers. "Are you trying to warn me about Bill, or make sure I don't end up hurting him?"

A sheepish expression crossed Leanne's face. "I'm sorry. It's just that the Bill you've described isn't typical. He's my best friend, but the way he acts around you is…different."

Zoe placed a finished package into a box. "My husband predicts that when Bill falls, he'll fall hard."

"And that would be the end of Paulson as we know him, according to *my* husband," Carly added.

Grace's insides twisted. She scooted back in her chair, disconcerted. "There's not going to be any falling for anybody, trust me. Bill is great, but if you had to guess the type of woman he'd fall for I'm sure it would be a snow bunny." Looking around the table, she saw the three women hiding their smiles. "As for me, I'm done with heroes. So we're good. No worries about anyone getting crushed. He's a friend, someone I'm happy I met. End of story."

* * *

In the alley behind the shop, Bill handed a case of wine bottles to Christian's cousin, Owen Slayter, who stood inside the delivery truck. Bill glanced at the back door of Welton Wines & Chocolates, wondering how Grace was doing.

He had no doubt his friends would make her feel welcome, but the women would be peppering her with questions. He didn't want anyone saying something that hurt Grace, even unintentionally.

Maybe he shouldn't have left her alone. But he didn't want to leave Owen to deal with loading the wine on his own.

Bill picked up another box. "This is going to be some reception."

"If you think there's going to be a lot of wine, you're right. But wait until you see the chocolates. My best creations yet."

"Leanne loves chocolate."

"Anything for my new cousin-in-law." Owen took the box from Bill and stacked it with the others. "I hear you have a houseguest."

"Two."

"A kid doesn't count."

Bill pictured Liam's hair standing straight up when he got out of bed. His impish grin when something intrigued him. His impromptu hugs, full of warmth when least expected. "This one does."

"I didn't know you liked kids."

"I love kids." Especially Liam.

"Riley Hansen said the mom is pretty."

"She is, if you like fresh-faced, natural types."

"My only type is someone new in Hood Hamlet. Other than the tourists and snow bunnies, it's slim pickings."

"There are a few available women you can date."

"The key word is *few.*" Owen stared off into the distance. "Christian got lucky with Leanne."

Christian might be younger, but he was strong enough to keep up with Leanne, on the mountain or off it. That was the kind of man she needed. "I'd agree with you there."

"You're the last of your crew who's unattached. When are you going to find yourself a wife?" Owen asked with an almost straight face.

An image of Grace flashed in Bill's mind. Not her smiling face, but a kiss-him-until-he-needs-a-cold-shower one.

"Who needs a wife when you can have an unlimited number of girlfriends?" He'd spoken those words before. This time they tasted sour. He didn't want to analyze why. "Are you and Christian still looking for someone to do your books?"

"We are. Part-time. In the New Year."

Bill thought about Grace. "I know someone with an accounting degree. Might be interested."

"Have them call or stop by after Christmas."

If she had a job here, she wouldn't need to go to Astoria except to sightsee. "Have your best man speech ready?"

"It's gonna go viral." Owen placed another case in the truck. "We're talking the sentimentality of a Hallmark card, humor of a stand-up comic and anecdotes of a bestselling memoir."

"You haven't started."

"No. I have two more days. Plenty of time to come up with something."

Bill's cell phone buzzed. He pulled it out, then read the text. Adrenaline pulsed through him. "Mission call out."

Swearing, Owen looked down at the leg he'd broken a little over a year ago. His injury had forced him and Christian to hunker down in a snow cave until OMSAR could reach them.

Bill tucked his phone in his pocket. "Sorry to leave you with all these boxes, but I have to go."

"No worries. I've got this." Owen's gaze met his. "Stay safe."

"Always."

Inside the shop, Bill approached Grace and the others. The women were wrapping and smiling and chatting. More than three quarters of the boxes had been done. "You've been productive."

"Grace wrapped over half of these," Leanne said. "She's amazing."

"Yes, she is." A warm sensation flowed through him. "We need to go. I have an hour to get my gear together and head to a briefing. Two climbers are lost."

Grace stood, grabbing her purse. "I'm ready."

"I didn't hear a text come in." Leanne fished her cell phone from her purse. "Yep. There's a call out."

Carly's face paled, whiter than snow. She gripped the edge of the table. "You can't go, Leanne."

"Of course I'm going." Leanne stood. "We need to put this stuff away."

Carly's lips trembled. Fear filled her eyes. "Bill…"

He knew exactly what Carly was thinking. Rather, who she was thinking about—her brother, Nick, and her fiancé, Iain. They'd died climbing two days before she was supposed to get married on Christmas Eve.

Bill touched Leanne's shoulder. "Sit. Finish the favors."

"Cut the crap, Paulson." Flames flickered in her eyes. "I have to go."

His gaze locked on hers. She wasn't going to like this, but he didn't care. "You may be the bride, but it's not a hundred percent about you. Stay here with Carly and Zoe."

A range of emotion flickered across Leanne's face. She scowled.

No way in hell was she going up the mountain two days before her wedding. "What would Nick say?" Bill asked her.

Leanne's eyes narrowed to slits. "Not fair."

His gaze didn't waver. He hated playing the Nick card, but she'd left him no choice. "I'm right."

Leanne pursed her lips. "Who knows what the mission is?"

Bill wasn't going to be swayed. "Doesn't matter."

"Christmas magic—"

"Didn't save my brother or fiancé," Carly interrupted with a firm voice. "I'm not superstitious, Leanne. But the timing is too similar. You do more than your share. Sit this one out."

Zoe touched Carly's hand. The two women had spent long hours, sometimes days, waiting for their husbands to return home from rescue missions. That bond was something Leanne wouldn't understand, since she was always out with the unit.

But Grace got it. Understanding and compassion shone in the depths of her eyes. She placed her arm around Carly's shoulder, proving what a special woman Grace Wilcox was, to comfort someone she'd just met.

Leanne didn't say a word.

She didn't have to.

Bill had been her best friend since they were nine. He knew that look as well as he knew his own reflection. She was not going to sit this mission out. The more they pushed her, the harder she would fight back.

Fine. Bill knew the one person who could talk sense into Leanne. Her fiancé wasn't a member of OMSAR, but Christian was a climber, and protective of his future wife.

Bill ripped out his cell phone. "Let's see what Christian has to say about this."

Panic flashed in Leanne's eyes. "You wouldn't."

Grace pressed her lips together, as if trying not to smile.

Bill tapped his phone. "Already calling."

Leanne dived for the cell. She missed his hand by an inch.

"Too fast for you, Thomas."

Her eyes grew steely. "Hang up. This isn't a discussion I want to have with Christian. He indulges me enough with my OMSAR responsibilities. I...won't go."

Bill tapped his screen. "I'll make sure you know what's happening up there."

Leanne cursed, sat and grabbed a favor box that needed to be wrapped.

"Looks like my work is done." He motioned to Grace. "Let's go."

Carly squeezed Grace's hand. "Thanks."

Grace's smile brightened her face, taking Bill's breath away. "You're welcome."

"It was great getting to know you." Zoe rubbed her lower back. "I hope we see you again before you leave town."

Grace looked at each woman. "I'll be heading out on the twenty-sixth."

Unless she got a job here. And he would have a vacancy in one of his rental properties in January. This might work out.

She stepped toward him. "Ready?"

The mission briefing. Bill had forgotten. That had never happened before.

He followed her out the door, ignoring the jingling bell and the way her hair swayed.

Grace messed with his head. And even though he wanted her to stay in town, he'd better make sure she didn't mess with his heart.

CHAPTER TEN

BACK AT BILL'S house, Grace watched him check his pack in the living room. Her admiration for him had tripled as she'd watched him handle Leanne. His compassion for Carly, unspoken but visible, showed the caring, protective man he was.

Bill Paulson had a big heart where his friends were concerned. Too bad he wanted to have fun, not find someone to be with for the rest of his life. He preferred multiple women. Not that Grace wanted to be one—or his one and only, if he changed his mind about settling down.

She glanced out the living room window with a sense of foreboding.

Snow fell from the sky, lighter than on Sunday night and Monday morning, but she couldn't imagine anyone going out in this kind of weather, let alone up a mountain.

No one but a hero.

Like Damon.

And Bill.

Her heart cracked, a mix of grief and anxiety spilling out. She pasted on a smile, something she'd perfected during video chats with her husband. "Almost ready?"

"Yes."

He pulled a strap through a buckle. The sound of nylon against plastic ratcheted her concern.

"It didn't take long." Nerves threatened to get the best of her. She rubbed her thumb against her fingertips. She would have preferred to pace, but that might disturb Bill. "You've got this down to a science."

"I've been doing mountain rescue since I was eighteen. It's second nature. But I recheck my gear to make sure I've got everything."

That was the most he'd said since leaving Leanne and her friends. Bill had been silent on the drive home, appearing preoccupied. When they'd arrived he'd said goodbye to his mom, put an exhausted Liam down for a nap, and then disappeared into the third bedroom, aka the gear room.

A deer outside the window snagged Grace's attention. Big, fluffy snowflakes surrounded the animal. The scene was pretty, but the snow was heavier, falling faster than sixty seconds ago.

She shivered and moved closer to the fireplace. Heat from the flames didn't take away the chill. She knew little about mountain rescue, but given the location and conditions, it sounded dangerous. "How long will the rescue take?"

"No idea, but I'm supposed to work tomorrow morning." Bill unclipped a carabiner from one loop and hooked it on another. "Depending on how the mission goes, I might not be home until Saturday. If you need anything—"

"Your mother gave me her phone number." Grace remembered the look of worry they'd exchanged before she'd left. On the way out the door, she'd told Grace to call her Susannah. "Your mom is going to stop by tomorrow. I'll—we'll—be fine."

Grace was fine now. Except for the churning in her gut, the goose bumps on her skin, the fear in her heart. She crossed her arms over her chest and squeezed tight, but didn't feel any better. She wouldn't feel better until she knew Bill was safe.

He glanced her way. "Don't let my mom get to you."

"What?"

He stood. "You seem worried."

"I am, but not about your mom." *Oh, no.* Grace cringed. She hadn't meant to let him know how she was feeling. Now wasn't the time to ask where the snow shovel was or get his opinion on her truck. She would figure those things out herself. Bill had more important things on his mind. "I mean…"

"I know what you mean, Gracie." He walked toward her, his tunnel vision focus gone. "Rescuer safety is the number one priority on any mission. No reason to worry."

"You must think I'm being silly."

He placed his hand on her shoulder. His gentle touch provided comfort and warmth, exactly what she needed. She fought the urge to lean closer to him.

Bill smiled. "Not silly. Sweet."

Don't go.

The words reverberated through her, so loudly she thought she'd spoken them.

But Bill remained smiling. Not his charming come-hither grin, or the you-know-you-want-me smile. This one was warm and sincere and affectionate. He'd looked this way at Liam, but never her. Not until now.

Grace liked that very much. She wanted to throw herself against his chest, have him wrap his strong arms around her and tell her everything would be okay.

What was going on?

Having a husband who'd deployed and trained for months at a time had taught her to be independent. Not always easy, especially as a newlywed and then a new mother, but she'd managed on her own. She'd had no choice after Damon died.

But to be feeling this way with Bill…

Her snow globe world tilted. Everything was shaken up. Turned upside down. Flooded by emotion and un-shed tears.

Uh-oh. Maybe Grace had fallen for Bill a little. That would explain her worry, right?

He tapped his finger on her forehead. "Tell me what's going on inside here."

Heat rose to her cheeks. "Nothing."

"Come on."

"It's just… Watching you get ready…" Grace chewed the inside of her lip. "I didn't know when Damon was going into danger. I never knew how he prepared for a patrol or what he was thinking when he headed out. He never talked about the details, what he saw or what he did. And I couldn't ask."

"You can ask me anything. Anytime."

She looked down. "I don't want to distract you. I'm sorry if I have."

"Hey, don't be sorry. I asked about you because I wanted to know."

"Damon rarely asked. If he did, he didn't press when I wouldn't answer." She rubbed her neck, thinking about their long-distance conversations. She'd been thankful for each minute. "I never wanted him to be distracted. I wanted to make sure he came back. But he...didn't."

Bill cupped her face with his callused palm. He stroked her cheek with his thumb. "I'm coming back, Gracie."

Her worry didn't disappear, but his confidence eased some concerns. "You better."

His hand was on her face, a half smile on his. "Trust me."

Grace had trusted him more than she'd trusted anyone else in the past two and a half years. She swallowed. "I do."

His gaze lingered on her, as intimate as a caress. He lowered his mouth and kissed her softly, a kiss full of affection and promise. He lowered his hand and stepped back. "I know you haven't given me your decision, but I couldn't help myself."

She mustered every ounce of strength not to touch her lips. "Take care and stay safe."

"Always." His smile deepened. He kissed her forehead, then slung his pack onto his back. "See you soon, Gracie."

He walked out. A few moments later, he backed his pickup out of the garage.

Touching her lips, Grace watched him drive away. The truck's taillights grew smaller until they disappeared into the snow-filled air. An icky, helpless feeling threatened to swamp her. She rubbed her arms, trying to chase away another chill.

It'll be okay, babe.

Grace sure hoped so, because everything felt wrong.

"Watch out for him, Damon. Please, watch out for him."

Inside Wy'East Day Lodge, the air buzzed with anticipation. Bill sat with Rescue Team 2 leader Sean Hughes and unit members Jake Porter and Tim Moreno at one of the long, cafeteria-style tables. Following the briefing with Sheriff Deputy Will Townsend, the four had been assigned on a team together. Like old times. Like when they went looking for...

Nick and Iain.

Bill downed the rest of his coffee. The liquid tasted like lukewarm sludge. He'd rather have a cup of the French roast Grace had brewed this morning.

Grace.

The thought of her brought a smile to his face. He hoped she wasn't still worrying about him.

I'm coming back, Gracie.

Damn straight he was. He had to make sure Liam got his white Christmas. Bill wanted to make sure Grace was...okay. And a few more kisses wouldn't suck.

Sean Hughes held a printout with the weather report. "Any questions on what we're doing?"

"Ride the snowcat, climb up, locate the two yahoos—I mean subjects—who failed to mark way points on their GPS going up to the summit, so now can't find their way down in a whiteout, then bring them back," Moreno said. "Pretty clear-cut to me."

Bill gave Moreno a nod of approval. "You should be the one giving the briefings."

Porter picked up his cup. "Seems like building some sort of shelter to block the wind would be prudent. Are we certain the two *subjects* haven't moved?"

Sean glanced up from the weather report. "According to tweets, the subjects have not moved."

"Tweets?" Bill stared, dumbfounded. "The dudes are on Twitter, talking about being lost in a whiteout and wasting their cell phone batteries?"

"Yes, but remember they're stuck, not lost," Sean corrected. "We have the GPS coordinates of their location."

Moreno swore. "Too bad we can't let the Twitter-verse talk them down."

"Not an option." Hughes pressed his lips together, not even a hint of a smile peeking through. The snowboard mogul had his game face on during rescues, but he was a casual kind of guy, who liked nothing better than to kick back with Zoe. "All we need is for them to fall."

Bill inhaled deeply. "Then it's up to us."

Porter nodded. "Let's get them down so we can go home to our lovely ladies."

An image of Grace, her hesitant smile and her concerned eyes, popped into Bill's head. He couldn't wait to get back home to her, show her everything was okay.

Moreno snickered. "Bill gets to go home to his mom."

Bill grimaced. "You're such a comic, Moreno."

"With you around, it's easy."

Sean glanced at the clock on the wall. He grabbed his pack and helmet. "Time to catch our ride."

Gathering his gear, Bill remembered how Grace had watched him get ready. Usually he had no problem pushing everything from his mind except the mission.

Not today.

He had always assumed his dad forgot about his family completely when he was away working. But maybe he'd thought about Bill and his mom back home.

Bill couldn't stop thinking about Grace. Her sweet smile, her nurturing heart, her hot kisses. She'd been worried about him, not wanting to distract him, yet curious about what he was doing. An adorable contrast.

He followed the others out of the cafeteria. "Do you tell your wives about our missions?"

Sean glanced back. "Zoe's an associate member, so she knows what we do. But she found some photos I'd taken of a body recovery.…"

Porter made a face. "Not good."

"I told her morning sickness made her throw up, not the pictures." Hughes stopped by the door. The snowcat wasn't there yet. "She didn't buy it."

"Smart woman," Bill said.

Moreno toyed with his gloves. "I'd love to tell Rita what we do, but she doesn't want to know anything except when I'll be calling it quits."

Bill shook his head. "Harsh."

"Yeah," Tim admitted. "But I love her. One of these days she'll drop the hammer and force the issue. I'll have to quit going out in the field, and plant myself at base operations."

Bill's mouth gaped. "Dude."

"Hey, she's my wife. Not much else I can do if she draws the line."

Grace would be different. She'd been married to an Army Ranger, a job way more dangerous than anything Bill did with OMSAR or the fire department. She probably wouldn't mind his mountain rescue work.

What the hell?

He did not need to be thinking about marriage.

It must be Leanne's upcoming wedding on his mind.

"Carly knows what goes on," Porter said. "She climbs, and grew up with OMSAR. If she wants to know specifics, I tell her. But usually she doesn't ask."

Bill double-checked the straps on his helmet. "Thanks."

"Why do you want to know?" Sean asked.

Bill shrugged. "Something Grace said before I left."

Jake's forehead furrowed. "The woman who's staying at your house?"

He nodded.

Sean let loose several four-letter words that would make a sailor blush. "If you're taking advantage of a woman, a widow, stuck in a difficult situation—"

"Chill." Bill raised his gloved hands. "We're just… friends."

Friends who'd shared some hot kisses, but no one here needed to know that detail.

Moreno made a noise that sounded like a half laugh,

half snort. "I know what you do with your so-called friends."

Sean's jaw hardened. "Keep your pants zipped with this one."

Bill laughed. "Interesting advice coming from a guy who left a trail of broken hearts until Zoe."

Porter grabbed Sean's pack and held him back. "Don't even think about it."

Hughes put his hands up. "You're right. I was that kind of guy before."

"Me, too," Jake admitted. "But once you meet that special woman, you change."

Hughes nodded. "You always say you don't want to settle down, so why do you care?"

"I don't care." Bill shouldn't have opened his big mouth. "Just making conversation."

"Good. Your reputation is worse than ours was," Moreno said. "Finding a woman to look past that won't be easy."

The snowcat lumbered toward the lodge.

Hughes opened the door. "Time to hit it, boys."

The frigid conditions smacked Bill in the face. The weather would make for a long day. If they didn't find the climbers, a longer night. But whether the two subjects were yahoos or just unlucky, they would be rescued the same as anyone else. OMSAR folks might joke or tease or argue, but that kept the mood lighter on crappy days like today.

The four of them crunched through the snow to where the snowcat rumbled, idling.

Bill loaded his gear, then climbed inside, followed by the others.

Sean Hughes squeezed in next to him. "Just giving you crap, Paulson. No hard feelings. But be careful. Women can be more beautiful and dangerous than a snow cornice."

Bill accepted the apology with a nod, but couldn't stop thinking about what his friends had said about his reputation. Regret was heavy and unexpected as the snowcat plodded up the mountain.

This was whacked. Bill shouldn't care what Grace thought of him going through women so quickly. He needed to get his head on straight. He loved everything about mountain rescue and going out in the field.

So why wasn't he focused on the mission? Why was he thinking about Grace, as if she was more important?

Hours passed. Daylight faded. Grace played with Liam, anticipating the sound of the garage door being raised. She fixed dinner, listening to the radio for updates. She put Liam to bed, wondering if she should call Bill's mom to see if she'd heard anything. He wouldn't be stepping on IEDs, or caught in a firefight, but the mountain held its own dangers with the cold temperatures, shifting snow and darkness.

Grace hate-hate-hated this icky feeling gnawing at her gut, turning her stomach into stone. Eating was difficult with no appetite. Sleeping, forget about it. Though Liam was fast asleep.

She had to do something besides sit and worry.

Grace paced the hallway, but that didn't help lessen

her anxiety. She checked the news again. The two climbers had been found and brought down, but she heard nothing about the status of the rescuers. Maybe cleaning would settle her nerves. She worked on the hall bathroom, then moved to the kitchen.

She scrubbed the counter, glancing at the clock on the microwave oven. Five minutes had passed since the last time she'd looked. She'd believed time couldn't go more slowly than it had during Damon's deployments. She'd been wrong.

When he'd been downrange, she'd never known what he was doing. A blessing, she realized. She had gone about her day with Liam, thinking, praying and worrying about Damon, sure. But that was different than waiting for Bill now.

Something clicked, a noise from the far side of the dining area.

She froze.

The sound came from the laundry room. The door to the garage.

Bill.

Grace released the breath she'd been holding.

Please be okay. Please be okay.

He stepped out of the laundry room. His hair was a tangled mess, in need of a wash and a comb. His face was dirty, with a streak of dried blood from a scratch on his cheek.

He'd never looked more gorgeous.

Her heart sighed. "You're home."

His tired eyes brightened. "I told you I'd be back, Gracie."

She nodded.

Bill opened his arms. "Come here."

She ran to him, threw her arms around his wide shoulders, hugged him tight and kissed him. Hard.

He tasted like salt and coffee. He smelled like a guy who'd spent the past ten hours climbing a mountain.

Grace couldn't get enough of him.

But this was more than she could take. These long hours had reminded her of how much she could bear. In her heart, she knew this was as much a goodbye kiss as it was hello. She pulled away from him.

Heroes were to be supported, honored, respected, whether on the front lines or first responders. But she couldn't love one. Not again.

He grinned. "That's what I call a homecoming. Let me shower and then we can pick up where we left off."

"Eat, shower and go to bed." She'd loved a hero once. She'd allowed his obligations for country, army and mission to come before her and their family. She'd put herself last and never said a word to him about how his priorities made her feel as a wife and mother. "You have to be exhausted."

"I'm good." Bill traced her lips with his fingertip. "Your kiss gave me new energy."

He lowered his mouth to hers.

She turned her head. "Let me heat you up dinner."

Grace headed to the kitchen. She liked Bill, appreciated his sense of humor, his kindness, his playfulness, but she had learned one thing watching him go off on his rescue mission. Her heart wasn't up for loving this particular hero.

No matter how wonderful he might be.

Bill followed her. "I'd rather taste you."

He wasn't making this easy. She removed the plate she'd made him from the fridge. "I'm happy you're home. Safe."

"I'm happy you're here. Safe."

Grace needed to make sure she remained safe. She placed the plate in the microwave, set the timer and hit Start. "I made a decision. About you and me."

He flashed her a charming, lop-sided grin. "Wasn't the kiss your answer?"

If only it could be… She took a steadying breath. "No."

"No to the kiss being the answer."

"No is my answer."

His face fell. "I don't understand. I thought…"

His obvious disappointment splintered her heart. "I was married to one hero. I can't get involved with another."

With a tender look that threatened to do her in, he tucked a strand of hair behind her ear. "Forget about being involved. Let's stick to kissing."

His lighthearted tone made it only worse. "We… I can't."

He leaned against the counter. "I need a better explanation than 'I can't.'"

She faced him. "Damon put his service first. Family was never his priority. I knew that going in, was okay with that, but I can't get involved with another hero, even…casually."

"I'm not like Damon. Not at all." Bill brushed his

hand through his hair. "I'm not proud of this, but I use the word *hero* so I can pick up girls."

As if a guy as gorgeous needed any lines. His killer smile could bring a woman to her knees. "You're still a hero. A firefighter and a mountain rescuer. You go when people need help."

"I'm doing my job. What I was trained to do."

"A hero is a hero. It's in your DNA. You put yourself at risk for others. Like Damon."

"There are a few risks, but we take precautions. It's not the same as being in combat. Damon was a patriot, one of the damn few out there willing to put his life on the line to preserve our way of life back home."

"What about when we needed him at home with us?"

"I can't tell you the number of times I thought the same thing about my dad. You made me remember something my mom told me. She said my father was working for us. That his job enabled us to stay in Hood Hamlet and live a good life." Bill held Grace's hand, his thumb stroking her skin. "You might not have felt like a priority, but did you ever think Damon was putting you first by fighting to protect you?"

"No, I never thought that. He was about honor and serving a greater good. Duty over love." Her throat tightened. She pulled her hand away. "I knew what he did was important, but I still felt neglected, like I didn't matter. Then he reenlisted. Said his Rangers needed him. When Liam and I needed him."

The words spilled from her lips. Words bottled up for years. Words she avoided because they were selfish, but not untrue. "Why can I say these things to you when I couldn't admit them to my husband?"

"Maybe you would if he was here."

"That's just it. I wouldn't. We served in the army together. We played our roles. I won't do that again."

"Then don't," Bill said matter-of-factly. "Enjoy Christmas and seven days of hot kisses with me."

The microwave timer buzzed. Grace removed the plate, grabbed a fork from the drawer and a napkin from the counter. She placed the items on the breakfast bar. "We'll stay for Christmas, but I can't..."

"Can't or won't?"

"Same difference."

"Not the same at all." He stood in front of her, his gaze intense and pointed. "I knew you were lots of things, Grace, but I never thought you'd be afraid."

She flinched. "What do you think I'm afraid of?"

"I have no idea, but I know fear when I see it."

"You don't know what you're talking about." She motioned to the plate of steaming food. "Eat."

"Thanks, but I've lost my appetite." He rubbed the back of his neck. "I'm going to bed. I'm working tomorrow, so I won't see you until Saturday."

Bill walked out of the kitchen without a glance back.

The house creaked. The wind howled. Grace shivered.

What did she have to be afraid of? She'd lost her husband. Her truck had been totaled. Except for Liam she didn't have anything else left to lose.

Well, except maybe her heart.

Not that Bill wanted her heart, only her...kisses.

CHAPTER ELEVEN

At 8:06 Saturday morning, Bill exited the station. The cold temperature stung his lungs. His boots crunched on the parking lot's snow. His gaze shot to Hood's summit.

Heading straight for Timberline sounded like his smartest move. Physical exertion on the climb up and the rush of adrenaline skiing down would help him forget.

Forget about Grace. Forget she didn't want him. Forget the feeling of helplessness of knowing nothing he did or said would change the way she felt.

I can't.

The two words stabbed at Bill. She would never be his. Disappointment weighed heavily. So did regret. He'd said similar words to women wanting to tame and domesticate him.

I can't date exclusively. I can't make a commitment. I can't be a family man.

His own words hammered his head and his heart. His dad couldn't seem to be a family man, but did that mean Bill should accept the same fate without at least trying? Maybe he could do more if he took baby steps.

Not that Grace would care if he tried.

A hero is a hero. It's in your DNA.

Bitterness coated Bill's mouth. Most women wanted to go out with firefighters because of their jobs. But Grace made wanting to help others sound like a vice, not a virtue.

He jumped into his truck.

Bill needed to wipe her from his memory bank. There were plenty of other women who wanted to date him. Why worry about the one who didn't? One who would be leaving him behind.

He turned on his left blinker, then remembered the envelope in his pocket.

Damn, Thomas.

Leanne had stopped by the station and asked him to make a "special" delivery. He thought the gesture was, well, misguided. But she was the bride, and he would do this for her.

A few minutes later he stood on his porch, eager to dart into the house, make his delivery, then escape. He opened the door.

Grace sat on the floor in front of the fireplace. She jumped, toppling a tower of blocks in the process. Colorful pieces flew across the room.

Liam leaped to his feet and ran, dragging Peanut. "Bill…!"

He closed the door, then swooped the boy into the air. "Good morning, little dude."

Grace remained on the floor, surrounded by blocks and other toys. She wore a pair of black track pants and a U.S. Army sweatshirt. Her hair was pulled back in a ponytail, and she had no makeup on her face. But she looked...beautiful. Too bad her lips were pressed together and her forehead wrinkled.

Bill's chest muscles tightened into a thousand tiny knots. He hated the anxious expression on her face.

Liam hugged him tightly. "Peanut missed you."

"I missed Peanut, too." Bill kissed the elephant, then looked back at Grace. Like it or not, he'd missed her, too. "Good morning."

The lines around her mouth deepened. "Hey."

He handed her the envelope. "This is for you."

She opened the flap and removed an ivory card with a vellum covering. "A wedding invitation?"

"Short notice, since Leanne and Christian are saying I do this afternoon, but they want you to attend." He set Liam on his feet and motioned to the blocks on the floor. Liam picked them up. "She would have delivered the invitation herself, but she's a little busy."

Grace reread the invitation. She didn't sound upset, more...amused. "Well, she is getting married."

"You'll go?"

Her gaze met his, her expression an unsettling mixture of worry and hope. "Liam."

"They've hired babysitters, so you're covered."

"I..."

Her hesitation hooked his heart, reeling him in. Forget skiing. He didn't need to be slogging up a glacier or speeding down one. The only place he wanted to be was with Grace and Liam. "The reception is being held at the community center, which has a preschool. The kids will hang out and eat popcorn and pizza."

Liam grinned. "Pizza. Pizza."

Her son's enthusiasm didn't seem to sway Grace. Bill would try to convince her. He didn't want to leave them, but staying home wasn't an option.

"Pizza's always good." He wanted to wipe the turmoil from Grace's eyes and put a big smile on her face. "The little dude's been stuck with adults since you got to Hood Hamlet. He needs playtime with other kids."

"Kids. Kids." Liam danced in a circle, waving his arms, wiggling his hips and kicking his feet. "I want to play with kids."

"Go, have fun, let loose. Thad will be there. Carly and Zoe, too." Grace couldn't say yes to more kisses, but maybe Bill could get her to say yes to the wedding. "Leanne appreciated your help the other day. She said there's no reason for you to be sitting home on a Saturday night when they have plenty of room, food and wine. Not to mention chocolates."

Grace reread the invitation. "I don't want to intrude."

"Leanne told me if you said no I'm supposed to kidnap you and bring you, anyway."

Grace's startled gaze flew to his. "She did not."

"She did. I'll do it, so you might as well say yes."

Liam crawled under the coffee table to reach the remaining blocks.

"Leanne and Christian want me there?" The uncertainty in Grace's voice matched the doubt in her eyes.

Oh, hell. Bill wanted to hold her. Hug her. Make her know she had friends in Hood Hamlet, a community, a home.

"They do." He might not get any more kisses. In less

than a week she would be gone. But they had tonight to laugh, eat, drink and dance. One night for the two of them. And a hundred other wedding guests. "I want you to go, too. With me."

"Go, Mommy, go." Liam climbed out from under the table. "We'll have fun."

"O-kay." She didn't sound as excited as her son, but she hadn't said no. "I'm going to have to find something to wear. My dresses aren't suitable for this weather."

"Let's go shopping." The words exploded from Bill's mouth like steam blasts from a volcano. He couldn't wait to see her in a clingy, sexy dress and heels. "There's a mall down the mountain."

Grace eyed him warily. "You want to go to the mall on the Saturday before Christmas to look at dresses? Do you want them to take away your man card?"

"My man card is safe. I'm always up for an adventure."

"The mall will be crazy."

"Crazy fun," Bill countered. "Santa's Workshop is there. What's Christmas without talking to the old guy in red?"

Liam jumped across the room like a kangaroo and pointed out the window to the figure in the yard. "Santa."

Bill grinned. "The decision has been made. Grab your coats and let's go."

A high school choir belted out Christmas carols near the mall's forty-foot, decked out tree. The chorus from

"All I Want for Christmas" stuck in Bill's head. All he wanted was to grab Grace and Liam by the hand, turn around and head back up the mountain.

If only Santa and his workshop could be found in an authentic ski chalet.

He hated how artificial everything looked. Overinflated, sparkly ornaments hung from the ceiling. Holiday sale notices plastered in every window and over every doorway begged for attention and customers. Automated holiday characters greeted shoppers, telling them to pick up their reward card at the mall info kiosk. Not that anyone rushing from store to store, juggling shopping bags, listened or noticed.

What had he been thinking, wanting to come here today?

He hadn't been thinking.

That was his problem.

Being around Grace short-circuited his brain.

She held Liam's hand.

Bill ran interference in front of them. If that made him "heroic," so be it. No one was going to bowl Grace and Liam over on his watch.

"Ready to bolt?" she asked.

"Nope." Bill wouldn't give her the satisfaction of being right. He touched his back pocket, where he kept his wallet. "Still there. That's a relief."

Grace's forehead creased. "What?"

"My man card." Joking might lighten his mood. He didn't go shopping at Christmastime, not unless you counted Freeman's General Store on Main Street and the gift shop at Timberline. "I thought someone might have taken it."

She beamed brighter than the shimmering snowman behind her left shoulder. "Remember, this was your idea."

"I take full responsibility for us being here. So where do you want to start?"

Liam pointed at Santa's Workshop, complete with fake snow, penguins, polar bears and North Pole sign. Inside the structure—built with unobstructed views on three sides to entice more children—the jolly old fellow sat on a huge leather chair, with a crying baby on his lap. "There's Santa."

Grace sighed. "Look at the line."

The queue of fidgeting families zigzagged between roped candy cane poles.

Coming today hadn't been Bill's best idea, but Liam was pulling Grace's arm out of its socket, trying to get closer to Kris Kringle. The least Bill could do was get them out of this crazy place quicker. "Why don't Liam and I wait in line to see Santa while you shop for a dress?"

Liam nodded like a bobble-head doll.

"You boys will do anything to get out of shopping," Grace teased.

Bill would much rather watch Grace try on dresses, preferably midthigh and strapless, with high-heeled, strappy shoes that showed off her toned legs. "I'm doing this for the little dude."

Liam pointed to himself. "That's me."

"I rarely get a chance to shop on my own." She

glanced at the line, then back at her son. "Will you be good for Bill?"

Liam nodded. "Always good for big dude."

"That's true," Grace admitted. "He listens to you better than he listens to me."

Bill stood taller. "I have the magic touch when it comes to kids."

"You do with Liam," she agreed.

As if on cue, tiny fingers laced with Bill's larger ones.

A protective instinct welled up inside him. He would do anything for the kid. No questions asked.

Bill squeezed the small hand entwined with his. "Come on, Liam. Your mommy has serious shopping to do. You can figure out what you want for Christmas while we stand in line."

"I know what I want." Liam's voice sounded certain for an almost-four-year-old.

Grace combed her fingers through his hair. "What, baby?"

Liam shook his head. "I only tell Santa."

Bill would get it out of the kid. "When you finish shopping, meet us here."

She looked at the people snaking their way around Santa's Workshop. "You'll probably still be in line."

He nodded. "I'll make it fun." Somehow.

"Santa." The kid pulled on Bill's hand. "Let's go see Santa."

After a few steps, he glanced back. Grace wasn't there. "So are you going to tell me what you want for Christmas, little dude?"

"Nope."

"I thought we were buds."

"We are. But it's a secret."

Bill could honor that. To a point. He would eavesdrop when the time came. He wanted to make this the perfect white Christmas for Liam and Grace. That meant finding them each the perfect present, even if he had to make a trip here tomorrow.

The kids in front of them must not have been too greedy, because the line moved quickly. Many of the children were well behaved—careful not to mess up their party dresses or buttoned-down shirts with ties—but Bill wouldn't trade any of them for Liam. His kid was as perfect as kids came.

Not his, he corrected with a surprising regret.

"Santa's taking a break to feed the reindeer," a squat elf with a Jersey accent announced.

The kids cheered at the word *reindeer*. The adults groaned.

With Santa out of sight, kids became impatient. Parents, too. Time dragged, like when waiting for high winds to die down so the ski lifts would reopen.

Liam didn't complain. He didn't make a sound, but stood quietly with his hands at his sides and his gaze focused on Santa's empty chair.

Bill whipped out his cell phone, unlocked the screen and pulled up a game. "Play with this."

Fifteen minutes later, Santa returned, walking with a cane. The line moved again. Not quite quick as a wink, they reached the front of the line.

Liam bounced from toe to toe, bursting with a sudden excitement. "Santa."

The kid's wonder made Bill grin like a fool. If dealing with the glittery facade of Christmas at the mall was what it took to see such awe in Liam's eyes, Bill was in. "We're next."

The elf from Jersey, wearing a pointy hat, ears and shoes, greeted them. He handed Bill a sheet of paper full of portrait options and prices. "Welcome to Santa's Workshop. What photo package do you want?"

Bill glanced at the sheet, expecting to see a handful of choices, not twenty-three.

The elf hovered, the scent of onions strong on his breath.

Liam grabbed hold of Bill's hand, inching closer with each passing second.

"A7." Not the most expensive one—no key chains—but the package had the most photographs and included two poses. Bill thought Grace would like more memories to hang on her walls.

Walls in Astoria.

He rubbed his temples to chase the impending headache away. Having a key chain to keep wouldn't have been bad.

"A7," the elf yelled to another elf behind the camera. "Go up and tell Santa what you want for Christmas."

Liam released Bill's hand, marched up the two steps and climbed on Santa's lap with no hesitation.

Brave for a three-year-old who had been frightened by the elf's loud presence, but not surprising, given the strong woman raising the kid.

"Ho, ho, ho." Santa's real beard was white and neatly trimmed. His blue eyes twinkled behind a pair of wire-rimmed glasses low on the bridge of his nose. His top-of-the-line red suit had a wide black belt with a shiny gold buckle. His black boots shone, as if polished that morning. Impressive for a mall rent-a-Santa. "Tell me what you want for Christmas, young man."

Liam cupped his hands around his mouth, leaned closer and whispered into Santa's ear.

Bill stepped forward, but he still couldn't hear.

Damn. He hadn't expected the kid to be so stealthy about his Christmas list.

Santa tapped his finger against his pink cheek. "That's a big request, Liam. Are you sure that's all you want for Christmas?"

Liam nodded. "Pos-i-tive."

"I'll see what I can do." Santa handed him a candy cane, then motioned to Bill. "Join us for a picture."

Another nod from Liam.

No way would he disappoint his little dude. The package did come with two poses. "Sure thing."

Bill positioned himself next to the chair. He placed a hand on Liam's shoulder.

"Smile at the birdie," the camera elf said.

Bill did.

Flash.

The light blinded him, filling his vision with dancing spots. He blinked. Once. Twice. Okay, that was better.

"What would you like for Christmas?"

He glanced around, then looked at Santa. "Are you talking to me?"

Santa smiled, the balls of his cheeks looking rosier. "Tell me what *you* want for Christmas."

Bill looked at Liam, who was examining a robotic polar bear. "I don't want anything. I have everything I need."

Santa adjusted his glasses. "Are you sure about that?"

"I bought new skis last month. I have more climbing gear than I could use in a lifetime. If there's anything else I need, I don't know what it could be."

"Search your heart." Santa sounded like a self-help radio personality. "That's how you'll figure out not only what you want, but what you need."

"O-kay." Bill tried to humor the old guy. Maybe Santa had been a psychologist and was now retired. "Later, Santa."

He walked toward Liam, who waited patiently for him by the exit.

"Bill," Santa called.

How did the guy know his name? That was odd. Bill hadn't told him. He glanced over his shoulder.

"Don't take too long to figure it out," Santa said. "Twelve days will be over before you know it."

The Twelve Days of Christmas didn't start until the twenty-fifth. Santa must have drunk too much reindeer juice during his break.

Bill picked up Liam, who waved at Santa. "Let's pay for your pictures, then see if your mommy found a dress."

At the photo counter, Bill glanced back at the workshop. Sure enough, Santa was watching them. The guy was taking his job too seriously if he thought Bill needed Santa's one-size-fits-all advice. Time to get out of there.

Liam held on to Bill. "Santa bring me what I want."

"What is that?"

"Not telling."

Grace stood ten feet away. She held a shopping bag in one hand and waved with the other.

Bill's heart thudded. Her smile drew him toward her like a bear to honey. She was just as sweet. Too bad he couldn't have another taste.

"How did it go?" she asked.

He handed her the white envelope containing the photographs and a CD with digital copies. "Great, except for Dr. Santa wanting to give life advice."

Grace made a face. "What?"

"Nothing." The old guy's words played over and over in Bill's head. Time to turn down the volume. "Let me guess. You found a dress."

"And shoes." Grace's face glowed. "Shopping was a real treat thanks to you."

Her words sent a burst of confidence through him. Maybe he could convince her to give him a chance.

"Treat. Treat," Liam chanted.

Grace laughed.

The bubbly sound seeped into Bill, making him feel toasty warm and a little buzzed, as if he'd downed a hot chocolate laced with a shot of peppermint schnapps.

He liked the feeling. He liked how they felt like a family. "Let's hit the food court. I'm buying."

Grace touched his shoulder for a nanosecond. "You paid for the Santa pictures. I'm buying."

"S-sure." He normally would have fought a little harder, except he wanted to know why the imprint of her palm burned his shoulder.

Maybe that whacked-out Santa was onto something.

Because there might be something Bill wanted for Christmas, after all—Grace.

"You look beau-ti-ful, Mommy." Liam sat on the edge of the bed. "You're green like a Christmas tree."

She hugged her son, getting a whiff of sugar and dirt even though snow covered the ground. Must be a boy thing, or he'd been playing in Bill's gear room. "Thank you. The color of the dress reminded me of Christmas."

"I like green. But blue is my favorite color." Liam hugged his stuffed elephant. "Peanut's, too."

"Do you want to take Peanut with you tonight?"

Liam nodded. "Bill said I could."

Bill. Grace smoothed the dress, hoping he liked it. Not that his opinion mattered. Well, maybe a little.

Which was ridiculous.

This wasn't a date.

They were friends. Nothing more.

"Are you going to wear your tags?" Liam asked.

Damon's dog tags. She kept them with her wedding band and Gold Star pin. "No, I don't think they'd go with my dress."

Grace had been wearing them less and less over the past few months. She hadn't put them on once since arriving in Hood Hamlet. But she had a feeling Damon didn't mind.

As long as she was happy and safe.

She'd felt that way here until Bill's rescue mission. Now she was counting the hours, waiting for the day after Christmas to arrive so she could leave. The longer she stayed, the less safe she felt.

A knock sounded. "Ready?"

Liam jumped off the bed and opened the door. "Look at my pretty mommy."

Bill's appreciative gaze ran the length of her. "Very pretty."

Heat rushed to her cheeks. "Thanks. You look… incredible."

Smokin' hot was a better term.

She'd never been swayed by a guy all dressed up and looking fancy. But in the black tuxedo and bow tie, Bill Paulson was the most handsome man she'd ever seen.

He tugged on his collar. "I don't know why anyone would choose to wear a monkey suit."

"To look suave and debonair," she said. "If the British need another MI-6 agent, you'd be the perfect man for the job."

Bill rolled his shoulders. "I feel like a penguin."

Liam giggled. "I like penguins."

Bill waddled around the room with his arms pressed against his sides.

Grace shook her head. "When someone gives you a compliment, you're supposed to say thank you."

He stopped moving. "Thank you."

"You're welcome." Bill not only looked like the next superspy, but he could be a groom. He was only missing his…bride.

She swallowed. Hard. "Are you a member of the wedding party?"

He adjusted his bow tie. "Groomsman and usher."

The way he fidgeted was cute. She would never have expected him to be so flustered getting dressed up. "Big wedding party?"

"Not too big. Christian's cousin Owen is the best man. His brother-in-law, Jeff, is a groomsman, along with me. Cocoa Marsh Billings is the matron of honor. She used to be Leanne's roommate. Christian's sister, Brianna, and Hannah Willingham are the bridesmaids. Hannah's three kids—Kendall, Austin and Tyler—are the flower girl and ring bearers. The fire chief is sitting in as father of the bride. He's always had a soft spot for Leanne, though he'd deny it to his grave."

The hearth-and-home aspect of Hood Hamlet was hard to ignore. "She told me she lost her family in a car accident, but found a family of friends in Hood Hamlet," Grace murmured.

"A few of us have." Bill's gaze lingered on her. "Your hair looks elegant."

"Thanks." She'd found a few accessories and bobby pins while searching through her boxes, enough to do her hair in a French twist. "I wasn't sure how to wear it when I couldn't find my flat iron. I'm sure it's in one of the boxes in the garage."

"The up-do looks good."

"I'm impressed you know what an up-do is."

"My best friend is getting married tonight. We are the only single ones left. That means I've been hearing about wedding and bride stuff for fifty-one weeks. That includes watching wedding shows."

"I'm surprised you haven't freaked out."

"Thomas provided lots of beer and food."

"That made all the difference."

"It wasn't my wedding, so I was good."

Of course he was. Bill was a confirmed bachelor. A player.

His words should make Grace feel better about not wanting to get involved temporarily. Instead she felt worse.

She looked at her shoes, a pair of sparkly, strappy heels. A total splurge. Impractical for the weather. A Christmas present to herself. She doubted women in Hood Hamlet would be wearing snow boots to the wedding, no matter the conditions.

"Nice shoes," Bill said.

She glanced up.

Mischief gleamed in his eyes. "I'm going to have to hold on to you tight so you don't slip on the sidewalk."

Liam nodded with a wise-beyond-his-years expression. "Bill never let me fall. You be fine, Mommy."

"That's right." Bill touched her son's narrow shoulder. "I'll take very good care of your mommy."

Uh-oh. Grace's tummy tingled with anticipation. The opposite reaction she should be having. Maybe she should have said no to the shoes and worn a pair of safe, bulky snow boots instead.

* * *

Leaving the vestibule and entering the church, Bill sneaked another peek at Grace. She looked stunning in the green, long-sleeved lace dress, which clung to her curves and fell almost to her knees.

Classy, elegant, sexy.

The hint of creamy skin through the lacy arms was hotter than any low neckline he'd ever seen. The slit up the back gave tantalizing glimpses of toned thighs. Much better than short hemlines that left almost nothing to the imagination.

With her hair up and light makeup on her face, he couldn't stop looking at her. Then again, his gaze strayed her way when she was wearing sweats and no makeup, too. She'd burrowed her way under his skin.

And he might not be the only one who felt that way.

He noticed men seated in the rough-hewn log pews glancing back, taking second and third looks at Grace. Thad craned his neck so badly he was going to hurt himself.

Protective instincts flared.

Bill placed his hand at the small of her back, possessively, as close to claiming Grace as his date as he dared. No one needed to know they'd come as friends.

Friends.

The word tasted sour, as if he'd gargled with vinegar to ward off a sore throat. But what could he do? Having Grace at the wedding, as his friend, was better than her sitting alone at home. Even if he might wind up playing bodyguard once the reception began.

Grace took a wedding program from a white basket. She glanced around, a look of awe on her face. "I love this church. Rustic yet lovely."

Trees with Christmas lights, poinsettias, roses and candles decorated the altar area. At the end of each pew hung boughs of pine and sprigs of holly tied together by red ribbons. Christian's grandfather was generously paying for the wedding reception. He'd suggested Timberline Lodge, but the community center held special meaning for Leanne and Christian and was their first choice of venues.

Bill and Grace reached the aisle. He extended his arm. "Bride or groom?"

"Bride."

He imagined Grace as the bride, wearing a flowing white wedding gown and a veil on her head, and holding flowers in her hands. She would walk down the carpeted aisle, like now, except he wouldn't be at her side escorting her. He would be standing at the front of the church by the altar, waiting for her to come to him.

What the...

Okay, he liked spending time with Grace and Liam. Hanging with the two of them was the closest thing to family time Bill had. But he sure as hell wasn't ready to have his own family.

No way.

Baby steps.

That meant dating.

The same woman.

More than once or twice.

Not flying off a cliff hoping the landing would be cushioned by powder.

He might not want to be like his dad, but he wasn't going to do anything stupid, either.

Especially not with Grace.

Not with Liam's white Christmas on the line.

Bill was not going to screw this up.

CHAPTER TWELVE

GRACE DIDN'T KNOW if Hood Hamlet's legendary Christmas magic existed, but something—maybe a smattering of holiday pixie dust—had turned the community center into an enchanted, romantic winter wedding land.

Votive candles surrounded the elegant red rose and pine centerpieces on white linen covered round tables. She sat at a table, the last person remaining after dinner and cake, caught up in the emotions of the surprising day.

Bill approached the table carrying two glasses of champagne. He gave her one.

Hood Hamlet's finest first responders from the sheriff's office, fire and rescue and OMSAR were in attendance. But not even the handsome bridegroom could hold a candle to Bill. Looking at him made her tummy tingle.

He sat next to her. "Enjoying yourself?"

"Immensely." She glanced around the room. Bright lights twinkled through white tulle gathered with holly and red ribbon. Star-shaped bulbs illuminated Christmas trees decorated with red hearts and white doves. The favors she'd wrapped were piled under the branches of two trees. Wedding presents surrounded the other trees. "The ceremony was touching. The reception is beautiful. Leanne and Christian are so in love."

"You like weddings."

"I haven't been to that many, but it must be wonderful to have so many family members and friends here to share their day."

The DJ invited the bride and groom to the wooden dance floor. A romantic ballad played. A spotlight shone on the happy couple.

Christian and Leanne danced, her white gown swishing with every movement. The groom twirled his bride under a sprig of mistletoe, lowered her into a dip and kissed her.

Applause erupted.

Grace sighed.

Bill raised his glass to the beautiful couple. "A special day indeed."

"I've never had second thoughts about eloping." Grace stared at the newlyweds twirling around the dance floor. "But experiencing the community and love surrounding Leanne and Christian today is pretty awesome."

The DJ spun another tune. Couples poured onto the dance floor.

Carly and Jake Porter. Zoe and Sean Hughes. Rita and Tim Moreno. Cocoa and Rex Billings. Sarah and Cullen Gray. Hannah and Garrett Willingham. Others joined in. She couldn't keep the names straight, but the smiling couples looked so in love.

Maybe something was in the water or the fresh mountain air.

Grace sipped champagne, trying to keep her gaze from straying to Bill.

The song ended.

"I want all the single ladies out on the dance floor," the DJ, wearing a red sparkly vest and matching bow tie, announced into the microphone.

Bill placed his arm on the back of her chair. "Aren't you going up there?"

She shrugged. "I'd rather let someone who wants the bouquet to catch it."

"I don't think that's how it works."

Leanne made her way through the crowd to Grace. "You need to get out there."

"The bride has spoken," Bill murmured under his breath.

"I've only begun, Paulson." Leanne's gaze challenged his. "You'd better be out there to catch the garter or you'll pay."

The two were like brother and sister. Even bickering, their love shone through.

Leanne pulled Grace onto the dance floor. "We have one more single lady."

"No holdouts allowed," the DJ said. "It's tradition."

Kendall, a young girl around thirteen or so, and a junior bridesmaid, rubbed her hands together. Her eyes twinkled. "I love traditions. Everyone in Hood Hamlet does."

Grace didn't know what to say.

Leanne stood on the DJ's platform with Christian at her side. She turned her back to the crowd.

No big deal. All Grace had to do was stand here and smile, and pretend this wasn't the last place she wanted to be.

The DJ raised his microphone. "On the count of three. One."

Women around her raised their hands in preparation.

Grace pressed hers to her sides.

"Two." The guests joined in the countdown. "Three."

Leanne swung her arm over her head, whipping the bouquet into flight.

The flowers flew through the air.

A woman in a silky purple dress jumped. Her fingertips missed the handle by inches.

Kendall rushed forward. She overshot the distance. The bouquet soared past her.

Right toward Grace. Her heart sank. She raised her hands to protect her face.

The bouquet hit them, dead center.

Darn. Grace gripped the handle.

Leanne beamed like a blushing bride should on her wedding day. She motioned for Grace to join her on the platform.

Grace forced herself to move, her steps dragging. Her feet felt heavy, as if she were wearing weighted moon boots that kept astronauts from floating off into space. That didn't sound like such a bad fate.

Guests watched her. Bill had to be watching, too.

The DJ gave her the once-over, then a nod of approval as if she'd passed his is-she-attractive-enough test.

Heat rose up her chest toward her neck. She couldn't remember the last time she'd been the center of attention in a crowd this big. Not since high school when, as the second in her senior class, she'd given the salutatorian speech at graduation.

The last time her parents had been proud of her.

The sweet scent of the roses tickled Grace's nose, bringing her back to the present. She clutched the bouquet like a life preserver, as if a plastic handle and a few flowers could save her from this fate. Nerves threatened to overwhelm her.

"Now let's get all the single guys up here, so we can see what lucky gentleman catches the garter."

Men replaced the single women on the dance floor, including Thad and Owen. Grace caught a glimpse of familiar brown hair.

Bill.

His gaze met hers. He smiled, an understanding I-know-you-hate-this-but-hang-in-there-it'll-be-over-soon smile.

Her heart stuttered. Her knees went weak.

Holding these lovely flowers, knowing what a wedding in Hood Hamlet could be like, she imagined him standing at the altar waiting for her to walk down the aisle, slipping a ring onto her finger, kissing her after being pronounced man and wife.

Heaven help her. She was falling for him. Falling hard.

She swallowed around the diamond-engagement-ring-size lump in her throat.

She may have already fallen.

Striptease music pulsed while Christian playfully removed a lacy blue garter from Leanne's thigh. The groom turned his back to the guests.

The semicircle of single men stood waiting.

"Remember, it's only slightly contagious, guys," Dr. Cullen Gray said, his arm draped around his wife, Sarah, a volcanologist on Mount Baker.

Sean Hughes held Zoe in front of him, his hands on her bulging stomach. He laughed. "But once you're infected, there is no cure."

"You won't mind." Rex Billings toyed with his gorgeous wife's long blond hair. "You might wish you'd come across the germs sooner."

Other guests heckled the bachelors.

"Are you ready, gents?" the DJ asked. "On the count of three. One. Two. Three."

Christian turned his back to them. He shot the garter behind him. The high trajectory took the lace-trimmed fabric toward some mistletoe hanging overhead. The garter hit the leaves, dropped straight down and landed on the floor.

No one moved for a second. Maybe two.

Thad and Owen reached for the garter at the same time.

But then Bill snatched it off the ground.

People cheered. Hollered. Booed.

Bill placed the garter over his biceps and took the

ribbing from friends like a good sport. His words from the night they'd met rushed back to Grace.

Most of my friends are married, but my life is good, and I'm happy. Marriage and kids can wait until those things change.

She couldn't believe he'd grabbed the garter, if that was how he felt. Granted, catching it or the bouquet didn't mean you *would* be getting married next. She sure wouldn't.

The two other men wanted the garter. Why had Bill picked it up?

For Leanne.

That would explain his actions.

"Time for another dance." The DJ started another romantic ballad. "The bride and groom will dance, and the two who caught the bouquet and garter."

Grace and Bill.

Maybe he'd picked up the garter so he could dance with her. Except…he'd danced with her already. She'd danced with Thad and Owen, too, so jealousy wouldn't have been a motive.

Bill held out his arm toward her. The smile on his face showed no regrets. "May I have this dance?"

Grace clasped his hand, liking the feel and warmth of his skin. "I believe the dance is tradition."

"You're catching on to how things work around here." The crinkles at the corner of his eyes deepened with his grin. He led her to the dance floor. "Tradition means a lot."

"Is that why you picked up the garter? Tradition?"

He glanced at the blue satin displayed proudly on his arm. "I wanted the garter because of you."

"Me?"

"You've danced with enough other guys. The rest of the night you're mine."

Mine.

"I'm staking my claim," he continued.

Grace wanted to be his. "With a garter?"

"Damn straight."

Her heart swelled with love for the man.

Love?

Oh, no. She'd fallen in love with Bill.

A man who didn't want to get married.

A man who wasn't ready to have kids.

A man who was a hero.

But this wasn't the same love she'd felt for Damon. That had been a sweet, mad rush of young love, the two of them taking on more than they'd bargained for at a young age, and making the best of things while they grew up fast. She felt a thrill and excitement with Bill, tingles and chills and heat, but something was different. They hadn't known each other long, but they felt like partners, able to talk, and support each other, rather than Grace trying to be the sole support of everything and figure things out on her own. Maybe age had matured her. Or motherhood.

Bill took her into his arms and wowed her with his fancy footwork.

They'd danced a fast song before, but she much preferred the slower tempo. "You're a great dancer."

"My mom made me take lessons." He twirled her.

"If you'd rather, we can hang all over each other like teenagers and rock back and forth while I try to grind on you."

Grace laughed. "I'd rather dance like this."

"Figured as much."

The lyrics spoke about one true love and forever. Two things she'd lost in the mountains of Afghanistan. Two things she wouldn't mind rediscovering on Mount Hood. She sighed.

"What?" Bill asked.

She didn't, couldn't answer.

The sound of silverware tapping on glass—the signal for the bride and groom to kiss—grew louder and louder.

She looked at Leanne, who pointed overhead.

Grace and Bill were dancing under the mistletoe.

She bit her lip. "What do we do?"

"Kiss."

Panic spurted through her. "We're here as friends."

Grace needed to be practical about things, about life. This wasn't a perfect snow globe world. Forget fairy tales. She wouldn't live happily ever after here in Hood Hamlet, even if the fantasy called to her in her dreams. "Friends don't kiss."

Not the way she feared she would end up kissing him—hard, passionately, in front of all these people.

He shrugged. "Blame it on tradition."

"Traditions. Christmas magic." She tilted her chin. "Is there anything else I need to know about Hood Hamlet?"

"Just kiss me, Gracie."

Her heart slammed against her rib cage.

The clinking of flatware against glass continued. The growing sound matched the roar of blood through her veins.

She wanted to kiss him, more than anything.

But should she?

Kiss me, Gracie.

Bill stood with Grace in his arms, a spotlight shining on them. His heart pounded in his chest. Adrenaline flowed, as if this were the crux of a climb, sketchy with a ton of exposure, not a slow dance at a wedding surrounded by friends.

Grace's soulful, brave eyes stared into his.

A vise tightened around his heart.

She'd been through so much. He'd wanted to let her decide about the kiss, not push her into one. But making her kiss him wasn't fair. Bill made his living helping people, rescuing them when needed. That was why he'd helped Grace in the first place. He had to help her now.

He parted his lips.

Grace rose up and brushed her mouth across his.

Heaven.

The touch of her lips against his rocked his world.

Heaven on earth.

That was the only way to describe her kiss, so sweet and warm and full of Grace.

He would never be able to get enough of her kisses.

Bill tightened his hold, not wanting her to get away.

She pulled back, ending the kiss as quickly as she'd started it.

A flame burned deep in his belly. His pulse raced. His lips ached for more kisses. For more Grace.

She smiled shyly, but her darker-than-usual eyes told him she'd felt the same pleasure and desire as him.

Wedding guests clapped. Someone whistled.

Bill heard the noise, but nothing could pull his attention from Grace. She was beautiful and courageous and in his arms.

Her eyelids fluttered. "We should keep dancing."

He would rather keep kissing, but danced instead.

Pride in Grace rocketed through Bill, filling every crack and crevice inside him, ones he hadn't known existed. "Thanks for playing along with another tradition."

Her nose crinkled. "Couldn't disappoint Leanne and Christian."

Bill didn't want to disappoint Grace.

"Didn't you see Leanne giving you the evil eye?" she asked.

Bill saw only the woman in his arms. "No."

His chest tightened. Ached.

He spun Grace to a corner of the dance floor. Her head dropped back her and her laughter filled the air.

Grace didn't want to be his. Okay, he got that. But he couldn't let her walk out of his life without taking wonderful memories of her time in Hood Hamlet.

When she looked back on her days here, Bill wanted her to smile and think fondly of this town, of him. He knew exactly where to start.

Grace and Liam deserved a memorable Christmas.

With a little help, he might be able to pull off something…magical tonight.

Leaving the Community Center, Grace didn't know whether to laugh or cry. Emotions flickered through her, like a light being turned on and off by Liam.

Bill carried her tired son in one arm and held on to Grace with the other. "That was fun."

"Amazing." Someone had shoveled the sidewalk leading to the parking lot, but she was careful with her steps. "I met so many great people. I didn't have to worry about Liam all evening. We danced so much my feet hurt."

So did her heart, but she didn't want to think about that.

"Your mom is a fantastic dancer, little dude."

"Yep." Liam didn't raise his head. He stuck his thumb in his mouth.

"He knows." Grace pulled up his hood so he wouldn't catch a chill. "We've danced around the house on occasion."

Bill slanted her a glance. "I haven't seen you dancing."

"You haven't been there the entire time."

"I'll be gone more this coming week."

"The holidays?"

He nodded. "I'm switching shifts due to the holiday. I'm off my regular shift on Monday, but working Tuesday, the twenty-fourth."

His words pierced her like an icicle falling from the eaves. A direct hit to her aching heart.

Alone. She and Liam would be alone on Christmas Eve. Again.

A heavy feeling soaked through her limbs, weighing her down. She nearly stumbled, and forced herself to pick up her feet.

It shouldn't matter if they were alone. She and Liam were used to spending Christmas alone. No big deal, right? She hated that every fiber of her being was shouting that it did matter. A lot.

Because she'd imagined Christmas in Hood Hamlet to be special, dare she say…magical?

Grace cleared her dry throat. "Do people usually switch shifts during the holidays?"

"It depends." He stopped on the corner. "I should be off, but Leanne usually takes the Christmas Eve shift so guys with families can celebrate at home. I offered to do it, since she'll be on her honeymoon."

"But you have a family." The words burst out of Grace's mouth before she could stop herself. "I mean, that's a thoughtful gesture, but you have your mom and dad."

"They'll survive until I arrive. I'm off at 8:00 a.m. My dad will be jet-lagged, so the festivities never start early. Besides, this won't be a typical Christmas Day."

"Because you have houseguests. Us."

"You and Liam are going to be the best part of my Christmas." The sincerity in his voice told her he was telling the truth. "But the annual Christmas afternoon snowshoeing trip I go on has been canceled. I'm bummed about that."

She could tell from the disappointment on his face. "What happened?"

"Too many people are going to be away." He looked down Main Street, with its myriad Christmas lights. "Leanne and Christian will be in Thailand. Hannah and Garrett in Seattle. Rita and Tim at her parents' in Portland. Zoe isn't feeling up to snowshoeing, and there's no way in hell Sean will leave her on Christmas Day even though her entire family is flying in from the East Coast for the holiday. That leaves me, Carly and Jake. So they…we…decided to cancel."

Nothing seemed to bother Bill except his parents, but this had. She squeezed his arm. "Snowshoeing on Christmas means a lot to you."

"What makes you say that?"

"You haven't talked that much about one thing since I've been here."

"Guilty." He half laughed. "We stopped going after Nick and Iain died. When Carly came back to Hood Hamlet six years later, we started again. I don't want us to end up with another mega-years hiatus. Sorry."

"No need to apologize." She wanted to make him feel better. "Find other people to go on your adventure. Then hang out with your parents. We'll be waiting when you get home."

"I meant to tell you. My mother wants you and Liam to join us for dinner on Christmas Day. If you have other plans…"

Liam pulled his thumb out of his mouth. "Nana."

Somehow Liam had turned Susannah into Nana. Bill's mom didn't seem to mind, and had started calling herself that when Liam was around. "I want to spend Christmas with Nana."

Frustration pricked at the back of Grace's neck. Being alone with her son on Christmas Day wasn't her first choice, but she didn't appreciate Bill bringing this up in front of Liam, getting his hopes up. She felt ambushed…trapped…forced to say yes. "No other plans."

Bill rubbed her son's head. "You'll get to go over to Nana's on Christmas."

"Yay." Liam stuck his thumb back in and closed his eyes.

"I kinda put you on the spot," Bill said to her.

Grace hadn't had to contend with someone else's input on plans in years. She crossed her arms over her chest. "Kinda?"

"I'm not good at this sort of thing."

"What thing?"

"The man and woman thing."

That must be his way of saying a relationship. She would be happy to put his mind at ease. "I'm not good at it, either. But there's nothing going on, so no worries."

In a few days she would say goodbye to the man she'd fallen in love with and this special town. Would her son remember the firefighter-mountain rescuer who came to their aid? Did she want him to remember?

The white lights on the giant tree in the center of town reminded her of stars. Wishing upon a star wouldn't help them. Even if Christmas magic existed, a relationship would never work.

Bill wasn't ready to commit to having a family.

Grace wasn't ready to commit to a man like him.

Shivering, she realized they'd walked in the opposite direction from the parking lot. "Can we go to the truck?"

"Nope," Bill said. "I have a surprise for you."

"It's cold."

"Not that cold."

"It's late."

"Nine o'clock is still early."

She rubbed her arms. "Not when you're three."

"Almost four," Bill and Liam said at the same time.

The two of them were so…

Don't go there.

Every muscle in Grace tensed. She was supposed to stay in Hood Hamlet until the twenty-sixth, but didn't know if she could last that long. Not when each moment with Bill felt so bittersweet. She couldn't leave now, could she?

Bill touched her son's nose.

Liam giggled.

No, she couldn't leave.

Not with Liam expecting to go to Nana's for Christmas dinner.

Bill nudged her. "Relax, Gracie. Trust me."

She'd relaxed. She'd trusted. She'd fallen in love.

Oh, boy. Listening to him again was the last thing Grace should do. She blew out a breath.

The condensation floated on the cold, night air.

Liam stiffened in Bill's arms. "Bells. I hear bells."

She listened and heard them, too. "Christmas magic?"

Bill pointed down Main Street. "A sleigh ride."

A sleigh with lanterns hanging off the side, drawn by a large chestnut horse, trotted in their direction.

She stared in disbelief and delight. No wonder they'd walked this way.

The sleigh pulled to a stop in front of them. The driver, wearing a black stovepipe hat and Dickens-style clothing, climbed down. He placed a step at the back of the sleigh.

Liam squirmed.

Bill set him on the ground. "Don't get too close to the horse."

The little boy stared in awe. "Wow."

Wow was right. Grace looked at Bill with a sense of wonder. She had no idea what he was doing, but a part of her was thrilled.

Bill took her hand. "Climb aboard."

She did. Liam followed, then Bill.

The bench seat was padded on the back and bottom. Comfy.

With her son between them, Bill covered them with wool blankets. "This should keep us warm on the way home."

"What about your truck?" she asked.

"Jake drove it to my house. Carly followed him."

Grace wanted to hug Bill, kiss him and tell him how she felt about him. But she didn't dare. "Thank you for going to so much trouble."

"No trouble at all."

The sleigh took them down Main Street and various side streets to see the holiday lights and decorations. They oohed and awed at the sights. Jingle bells provided the backdrop music.

Grace looked at Bill, overcome by her love for this man who would do something so special for her and Liam. She sniffled, holding back tears of joy and a few of regret. "This is so wonderful."

"Cold?" Bill asked.

"A little."

He added another blanket on top of them, placed his arm on the back of the seat and drew them toward him. "Better?"

She relished the feel of his arm around her. "Perfect."

And it was.

Tiny snowflakes fell from the sky, the final touch to an enchanted evening.

She looked back and caught a flake on her tongue. Bill laughed. "Christmas magic."

Her gaze met his. "Who needs Christmas magic when we have you?"

Too bad tonight couldn't last…forever.

Too bad this couldn't last.

Bill kept the days leading up to Christmas full of holiday fun. Breakfast with Santa. The light display at the Portland International Raceway. Sledding at the sno-park. Making gingerbread houses with Carly, Jake and Nicole.

Skiing hadn't entered Bill's mind, even though he'd ended up with Monday off, too, due to switching shifts.

All he wanted was to spend as much time with Grace and Liam as he could. That satisfied him as much as being on the mountain, but in a different way. Bill loved Leanne like a sister and never thought he'd be closer to any other woman besides his mom. But with Grace, he'd found something more, someone who not only understood and accepted him, but also made him want to be a better man.

Each day brought the twenty-sixth closer. His collar kept tightening, but what could he do?

CHAPTER THIRTEEN

THE EARLY HOURS of Christmas Day arrived with a fresh snowfall and a two-alarm house fire. Bill preferred busy shifts, but not like this. Fortunately, the fire was contained quickly, with no injuries or casualties.

No doubt Christmas magic at work.

Back at the station, he showered, then lay in his bunk, trying to sleep. But he couldn't stop thinking about Grace and Liam. Last night, his mother had texted him that she and his dad had taken Grace and Liam to Christmas Eve services at church and then out for dinner.

A nice gesture by his parents.

He hoped nothing had gone wrong.

Someone snored in the room next door—O'Ryan.

Bill's father had arrived yesterday, on Christmas Eve. No doubt he'd driven straight to the mall to do his Christmas shopping. But then again, several of the firefighting crew had stopped by the general store after lunch. Even Bill had picked up a couple things. Maybe he should cut his dad some slack.

Bill looked at the clock: 4:02 a.m. All he could think about was Grace.

Grace. Grace. Grace.

She was on his mind constantly.

He wanted to give her everything, not because she'd lost her husband or been through rough times, but because he wanted to see her laugh and smile and enjoy life. He didn't want her to look as if she was waiting for the next bad thing to happen. The way she'd looked when he'd answered the door eleven days ago.

But Bill didn't know how to start. Because he had no doubt he would fail.

His stomach churned. Maybe he shouldn't have eaten so many brownies for dessert.

A medical call at six o'clock woke the station.

At eight o'clock, Bill looked at the next shift like a Get Out of Jail Free card. He didn't hang around the station. He didn't want to hear who got what for Christmas. No one minded when he cut out a few minutes into the briefing. He wanted to get home and see Grace and Liam.

The kid had been so excited about Santa coming. Porter and Hughes had offered to climb on the roof last night and leave footprints and reindeer droppings. Liam must be bouncing like a ball this morning, thinking Santa had been there.

Filled with anticipation and excitement, Bill pulled into the driveway.

A crossover SUV was parked on the street in front of his house. Must be Grace's new car. Used, but with low mileage according to Thad, who had called Bill yesterday and said that Grace had reluctantly signed over the truck and taken the settlement from the insurance company. Together, Thad and Bill had come up with a way to help her.

His parents' car was parked on the street behind the SUV.

Bill quickened his pace, his boots sinking into the snow. He opened the front door.

The aromas of coffee, bacon and something baking hit him first. A Christmas carol played. Peals of laughter filled the air.

Liam.

Grace.

Sweet music to his ears.

Bill closed the door. He expected to see Liam running toward him, and a mess of torn wrapping paper, discarded bows and empty boxes.

The little dude was a no-show. All the presents were still under the tree, gifts wrapped in brightly colored paper and tied with pretty ribbons. Stockings stuffed with goodies hung from the fireplace.

He stared, dumbfounded. It was Christmas morning. He glanced at the clock: 8:07. But nothing had been opened.

Realization pummeled Bill in the gut.

They were waiting for him to get home.

He could understand Grace doing that, but Liam? Talk about sheer torture for the poor kid.

Bill stood at the doorway to the kitchen and dining area.

His mother and Grace were in the kitchen, cooking breakfast—eggs, bacon and something delicious-smelling in the oven. Both women wore aprons and chatted, but as always, Grace drew his eyes and touched his heart.

The swing of her hair and the smile on her face sucked the breath out of him. Caring and genuine and strong… She didn't need him or any man to rescue her. She was doing fine on her own.

His father sat with Liam at the dining room table, smiling, talking and building a wall with big LEGOs. His dad's hair had grayed since the last time he'd been home, in the spring. His face was tan, but his wrinkles were deeper. His eyes looked tired, but full of warmth gazing at Liam.

Bill couldn't believe his dad was playing with the little dude. His father had never spent time like that with him, but he couldn't be happier for Liam. The kid deserved all the attention and love he could get.

Affection for the little dude threatened to swamp Bill. He never knew he could care so much for a little kid and a woman.

Not just any woman.

Grace.

These four people were his family.

Bill clutched the door frame, overcome with emotion.

He remembered what the mall Santa had said.

Search your heart. That's how you'll figure out not only what you want, but what you need.

Bill had searched his heart. The answer kept coming up the same. He wanted Grace and Liam more than anything else in the world. They deserved better than him, but he needed them.

He loved Grace. He loved Liam.

Bill loved them with everything inside him. He had to make this work.

He'd learned from his dad what not to do. Don't leave your family alone. Bill had learned from years of dating what he didn't want. A night or two with blend-together women.

No one had forced him to be like his dad, and he wasn't. Not really. Bill might like adventure, but he was dependable, devoted to his mom and rooted in Hood Hamlet.

No one had forced him to date all those women. He'd stopped. He hadn't spared one glance or thought about another woman since Grace had entered his life.

But was it enough?

Santa had said something else.

Don't take too long to figure it out. Twelve days will be here before you know it.

Not the Twelve Days of Christmas.

The twelve days Grace was planning to stay in Hood Hamlet.

Today was day eleven.

Hope poured through Bill. He still had time.

He had no idea how to convince a woman like Grace to take a chance on a guy like him. But he had to do something. Make promises. Kiss her. Hold her boxes in his garage hostage until she agreed to stay. He would try anything.

What was the worst thing that could happen?

She could say no. She likely would say no. Break his heart. Leave for Astoria. And he'd be miserable.

But the same thing would happen if he didn't try. If he let her go without asking her to stay, he would regret it for the rest of his life.

Come on, Christmas magic, don't let me down.

He took a deep breath, gathered his strength and mustered his courage. "Merry Christmas."

His mother greeted him with a smile. Grace, too.

Liam scampered out of his chair and flung himself against Bill's leg.

His father stood. "Good to see you, son."

Bill touched Liam's shoulder. "Welcome home, Dad."

"Give Bill a chance to say hello to his father." Grace opened the lid of the cookie jar. "You can have one of Nana's cookies."

Liam ran into the kitchen.

Bill's dad hugged him. "A lot's happened since I was here last. You're not the same kid."

Bill glanced toward the kitchen, at Grace and Liam. "Everyone has to grow up sometime."

"That's what your mother said last night." His dad smiled softly. "I always knew you'd be a much better father than I ever was to you. Maybe I'll do better being a grandpa."

Regret and insecurity filled his voice. If Bill had ever doubted his father's love, he didn't now. A lump burned in his throat. "You'll do fine. I know you did the best you could."

"It was easy to let your mom do everything. She's such a strong woman and never seemed to need me around. You're just like her." Pride gleamed in his father's eyes. "I never had to worry because I knew you were there for her when I couldn't be."

"I'll always be here. For both of you." An unfamiliar contentment settled over Bill. He looked at Liam. "Who wants to see what Santa brought?"

Best. Christmas. Ever.

Grace sat on Bill's couch, watching him and Liam play with her son's new train set. The house was a mess, but she didn't care. No one did. They could clean tomorrow.

Bill's dad handed her a mug of spiced cider. Neil Paulson looked like an older version of his son, handsome and athletic. "Enjoy, Grace."

From today on, the scent of cloves and allspice would remind her of Christmas morning and Bill. "Thanks."

His father smiled. "Children make Christmas so special."

"Yes, they do." This was the first Christmas since Damon's death that she'd enjoyed herself. The past years she'd gone through the motions for Liam's sake. She'd been waiting for the normal grief to come, but so far it hadn't.

Progress. Maybe.

Or maybe her happiness had to do with being in Hood Hamlet with Bill. Grace wished Christmas magic could make things work between them. She would allow herself the luxury of wishing and daydreaming today. Tomorrow, when she packed her bags and left for Astoria, she would have to be practical.

The train chugged around the tracks, whistle blowing.

Liam placed his stuffed animal in one of the cars. "Peanut wants to go for ride."

Grace snapped a picture.

Bill's gaze met hers, sending her pulse racing. No matter how many times she told herself not to react to him, she still did.

"You haven't opened your present from me," he said.

"I can open it now."

"It's not under the tree." Standing, he looked at his parents. "Will you watch Liam?"

"Happily." Susannah beamed, waving her hand. "Take your time. We're fine here with him."

Bill led Grace to the garage. "Close your eyes."

She did.

A door opened.

She wiggled her toes in anticipation.

He led her down a step. "You can look now."

Damon's truck minus much of the front end was tied with the biggest red ribbon she'd ever seen.

She gasped, covered her mouth with her hands. "The truck was totaled. I used the settlement for a down payment on the car."

"Thad bought the salvage rights, then sold them to me." Bill placed his hand at the small of her back and led her closer. "It still needs a lot of work, but we'll get the truck running again. Not that you need two vehicles, but I thought you might…"

His voice trailed off.

"It's the perfect gift." Tears stung her eyes at his thoughtfulness. "You have no idea."

"Anything for you, Grace."

"Thank you." She hugged him, soaking up the strength and smell of him. She didn't want to let go, but self-preservation sent her backing out of his arms. "Thank you so very much."

"I'm happy to keep the truck here," Bill offered. "So Thad can work on it."

"That would be great." And would give them a reason to keep in touch. Okay, now she was being silly.

"I was thinking you might want to forget about Astoria and stay here."

His words filled her with hope. "You want us to stay?"

"It makes the most sense," he said. "Astoria is a nice place, but you don't know anyone there. You have friends in Hood Hamlet. People who care about you and Liam."

"People."

"Me, Grace. I care. I want you and Liam to stay."

She opened her mouth to speak, but no words came out.

"Hood Hamlet is a great community. I have rental properties. You and Liam could move into one. A house with a yard. Get a dog or a cat. Or both. You won't have a view of the Pacific Ocean, but you'll have Mount Hood."

Everything he said was valid. But where did Bill and his caring for them fit in? "I love it here, but—"

"I want you to stay because I need you to stay."

Her heart pounded so loudly she was sure everyone in Hood Hamlet could hear it. "I'm touched."

"We'll make this work. I'll do whatever it takes."

He was so sweet. This was breaking her heart. "I..." She didn't know what to say.

"You will always be first with me." His breath hitched. "I love you. I love Liam, too."

The unexpected words shot through Grace, filling her with a mix of conflicting emotions—happiness, fear, joy, regret. Knees weak, she leaned against the truck.

"I thought my life was perfect. Then you and Liam showed up on my doorstep that night, frozen and wet and hurting." The sincerity in Bill's voice bruised her heart more. "I thought I was helping you, but you and Liam were the ones helping me. I never thought I wanted a family, but thanks to you I realized what *perfect* is all about. You. Me. Liam. A family. We belong together."

She closed her eyes, afraid that if she opened them, all this—his words, Bill himself—would vanish. "I want to believe this could work."

"Believe, Gracie."

"I wish I could." But something was holding her back. "I'm scared. You were right about me. I'm afraid."

"That makes two of us, because you scare the hell out of me, Gracie."

The door to the kitchen swung open suddenly. "Get in here," Neil all but shouted.

Bill's gaze met hers.

"Liam," they said at the same time.

Bill grabbed her hand, and they ran to the living room.

Liam sat by the tree with two stacks of ripped pieces of wrapping paper.

Seeing her son brought a wave of relief. She'd thought something had happened to him. "What's going on, baby?"

He raised his chin. "Time for more presents."

"We'll continue our talk later," Bill said to her, then joined him on the floor. "What are these?"

Liam picked up the first pile of wrapping scraps. "This one is for Mommy."

"How sweet." She'd never gotten a present from him. This was the first Christmas in years she'd had packages with her name on the tag that she hadn't purchased. "I wonder what it could be?"

"Open it, Mommy."

Grace unwrapped the gift, pulling off scrap after scrap of paper until she came across the back of an envelope. She turned it over. The word *Free* was scribbled in the corner where a stamp would go. Her name and address in Columbus and an APO AE address were written, too. She knew the handwriting as well as her own.

Damon's.

Her heart lurched. Her hand trembled.

Bill grabbed hold of her. "Grace."

"You're so pale, dear," Susannah said.

Neil held out the throw from the couch. "Would you like a blanket?"

She looked at her son. "Liam…"

He smiled. "Read it, Mommy."

Her fingers shook as she unsealed the envelope. She removed a familiar looking sheet of paper. She'd sent Damon the stationery in her last care package. She unfolded the letter and read the date aloud.

Her world exploded. Or maybe it was her heart. All she knew was this, whatever this was, had been written right before Damon had been killed.

Her vision blurred. She lowered the letter. "I—I can't."

"I will." Holding her with one arm, Bill took the paper and read:

"Dear Grace,

"Thanks for the care package. Once again you prove to be the best army wife ever. You always know what to send me. The other night you sounded sad. I know it's hard to be apart. You tell me to stay safe, and I'm trying. I want to come back to you and our son more than anything in the world.

"But what I'm doing over here, it's for you, babe. I know you think I love my job. I do, but not as much as I love you. Every day I spend away from you and Liam is a day I've spent protecting you. Keeping you safe. Making sure no one hurts the two people I love most. You're the reason I'm here. You and Liam.

"So always remember…it'll be okay, babe. No matter what's going on, I'm here for you. Whether I'm at home or a world away. I love you and I always will.

"Your angel downrange,

"Damon"

Liam sat with Peanut on his lap.

Bill's eyes glistened, as did his parents'. He handed Grace the letter.

She silently read Damon's handwriting. His words.

"I was so wrong. All this time I thought he'd put everything else ahead of us." But Damon hadn't. For so long she'd believed his being a Ranger was the most important thing in his life, not her. She looked at Bill. "But you were right about him. You didn't even know him, but you knew."

"Damon did what he did out of love. That's how I knew." Bill cupped her face with his hand. "Because I feel the same way about you and Liam. I'm not Damon. But I love you guys. I will do anything I can to keep you safe."

It's okay now, babe.

She could almost hear Damon's voice in her head and in her heart. The heaviness inside her lifted, replaced with a peace she hadn't thought possible.

Yes, it was okay now.

Grace wasn't afraid to love a hero. She'd been terrified of losing another and having to face that deep, dark pain again.

But now she knew.

Loving was worth the risk, the hurt, the heartache. She would rather have had five days with Damon and lost him than to never have been with him. She could acknowledge her fear and forge ahead. Bill might not come home from a shift or a mission, but she couldn't let that stop her from being with and loving an incredible man. "I love you."

"I love *you*." Bill lowered his head and kissed her, a kiss full of tenderness, warmth and love. Slowly, he pulled away, then sat next to Liam again. "So here's the deal, little dude. I want to ask your mom to marry me. We can't get married right away, since we just met and I don't have a ring. But that means you'll have to stay in Hood Hamlet. Since you're the man of the house, I wanted to ask your permission. Is it okay, Liam?"

"It's fine, Daddy."

The two hugged.

Grace covered her mouth with her hands.

Bill's parents' embraced.

Liam handed Bill a present wrapped in scraps. "This is yours."

"Thanks, little dude." He peeled away the pieces of paper. "It's a ring box."

Grace gasped. "Where did you get the presents, Liam?"

"Santa," he said without any hesitation.

Santa. Great.

Bill opened the box. "Whoa."

A beautiful diamond flashed and sparkled, as did the smaller diamonds inlaid along the gold band.

"I have a feeling it'll fit you, Grace," Susannah said.

Grace had the same feeling.

Bill handed her the box. "Nice ring."

"Gorgeous." Grace turned the box over and recognized the name imprinted in gold. She couldn't breathe. "It's from a jewelry store in Columbus. Bill..."

He nodded. "So, Liam, what did want Santa to bring you this year?"

"A daddy." Liam smiled proudly. "You."

Grace's heart melted. Now she knew why Liam wouldn't tell anybody what he wanted for Christmas.

"That's awesome. You got what you wanted," Bill said. "But where did the letter and ring come from?"

Liam bounced Peanut. "I told you. Santa."

Grace joined them on the floor. "Santa gave them to you?"

"He helped me find them," Liam said.

"When?" she asked.

"Last night. I get up. You sleep."

Bill had told her about his friends coming over to make Christmas Eve more real for Liam. "I did hear something on the roof," she said.

"Santa come down the chimney," Liam said. "Angel says to go to truck. We find these."

Grace was afraid to ask. "Angel?"

Liam nodded. "Santa needed help. Angel help. I help, too."

She couldn't think straight. Letters and a diamond ring didn't magically appear. "Can you show us where you found them?"

In the garage, Liam pointed to a latched cubby in the backseat of the truck. "Ring was in here."

Oh, Damon. Grace took deep breaths so she wouldn't lose it. He would have returned from Afghanistan in time for their anniversary. Was the ring supposed to be her present? "Damon must have hidden the ring so he could give it to me when he returned home."

"What about the letter?" Bill asked.

Liam pulled a small rectangular box from under the backseat. "The letter was in here."

"I've never seen that before." She opened the lid. Letters and postcards she'd sent Damon during his last deployment were stuffed inside. A few blank envelopes and folded pieces of paper were on top—the same stationery he'd used to write her letter. "This must have fallen out of his things that were returned to me."

"Peanut hungry," Liam announced.

Susannah took his hand. "Nana will get you something to eat. And Papa will help."

The three returned to the house.

Grace waited for the door to close. "I keep trying to figure out how this could have happened."

"Maybe Liam found the items on his own," Bill suggested. "He's spent enough time in the backseat."

"That seems like the most logical explanation. When did the truck arrive?"

"Late last night. Hughes and Porter helped Thad before they went onto the roof."

"I heard them." Grace smiled, thinking about his friends pretending to be Santa. "The jingle bells were a nice touch. It sounded like Santa was coming down the chimney."

Bill's forehead wrinkled. "They didn't have jingle bells or do anything with the chimney."

"But—"

"If it wasn't them…"

Then it was someone else. Santa. And an angel.

She looked at the box of letters in her hand and the ring box in Bill's. "No way."

"What other explanation is there except for Christmas magic?"

The emotion in his voice brought tears to Grace's eyes. "You really think Santa and an angel and Christmas magic played a part in this? Not Liam?"

"Why not?" Bill tucked Grace's hair behind her ears. "This is Hood Hamlet. Anything can happen in December."

She took a deep breath. "I don't know."

"Sometimes you *don't* know. You can't always be certain. You have to take a leap of faith and just believe." He caressed her face. "Can you believe?"

"I want to."

"That's good enough for me." He handed her a jacket with the word *Rescue* printed on the sleeve. "Put this on."

"Why?"

He pressed the garage door button. "I don't want you to be cold."

Taking her hand, he led her out of the garage to the Santa statue in the front yard. "This seems like the perfect spot."

Snow fell from the sky, landing on their hair and

shoulders. Grace felt as if she were standing inside a snow globe. "For what?"

"We haven't known each other long, but I have Liam's permission. And I want yours." Bill dropped down on one knee. "I love you, Grace Wilcox. Will you marry me?"

Grace wasn't sure what had happened here in the early hours of Christmas morning. She wasn't sure she wanted to know. But she couldn't mistake the joy and love overflowing from her heart. "Yes, I'll marry you."

Bill stood up and brushed his lips over hers. "Forever, Gracie."

Forget being inside a picture-perfect snow globe. Real life—real love—was so much better. She stared up at her hero, at her future. "Forever."

* * * * *

#4403 SECOND CHANCE WITH HER SOLDIER
Barbara Hannay
When Corporal Joe Madden returns to his estranged wife, Ellie, he wants her signature on the divorce papers. But stranded together in bad weather, could a Christmas truce bring the sparkle back into their marriage?

#4404 SNOWED IN WITH THE BILLIONAIRE
Caroline Anderson
Childhood sweethearts Georgia Beckett and Sebastian Corder are each other's refuge in a blizzard. Is it time to give their love a second chance?

#4405 CHRISTMAS AT THE CASTLE
Marion Lennox
When Angus Stuart offers Holly McIntosh the *temporary* position of chef in his castle, she's determined to make it permanent. Can she melt the Earl's brooding heart?

#4406 SNOWFLAKES AND SILVER LININGS
The Gingerbread Girls
Cara Colter
When Casey Caravetta meets Turner, her ex, at a Christmas wedding, it *doesn't* inspire much festive cheer. But maybe a little bit of holiday magic is just what they've been waiting for....

**Celebrate Christmas next month with Cara Colter's
Snowflakes and Silver Linings, the third and final story
in the sparkling Gingerbread Girls trilogy!**

Turner Kennedy had seen her as no one else ever had. But
she had seen him, too, felt she had known things about him.
Now, studying his face as he squinted up toward the porch
ceiling, she put her finger on what was different about him.

During those playful days, Turner Kennedy had seemed
hopeful and filled with confidence. He had told her about
losing his dad under very hard circumstances, but she had
been struck by a certain faith in himself to change all that was
bad about the world.

Now Casey was aware she was looking into the face of a
warrior—calm, strong, watchful. Ready.

And also, deeply weary. There was a hard-edged cynicism
about him that went deeper than cynical. It went to his soul.

Casey knew that just as she had known things about him
all those years ago. It was as if, with him, she arrived at a
different level of knowing with almost terrifying swiftness.

And the other thing she knew?

Turner Kennedy was ready to protect her with his life.

A second passed and then two, but they were long, drawn-
out seconds, as if time had come to an amazing standstill.

This was what chemicals did, she told herself dreamily. He
thought, apparently, they were in mortal danger.

She was bathing in the intoxicating closeness of him.

Casey could feel the strong beat of his heart through the thin fabric of his shirt. He was radiating a silky, sensual warmth, and she could feel the exact moment that his muscles began to uncoil. She observed the watchfulness drain from his expression, felt the thud of his heart quieting.

Finally, he looked away from the roof and gazed intently down at her.

Now that his mind had sounded some kind of all clear, he, too, seemed to be feeling the pure chemistry of their closeness. His breath caressed her face like the touch of a summer breeze. She could feel her own heart picking up tempo as his began to slow. His mouth dropped closer to hers.

The new her, the one who was going to be impervious to the chemistry of pure attraction, seemed to be sitting passively in the backseat instead of the driver's seat. Because instead of giving Turner a much-deserved shove—fight—or scooting out from under him—flight—she licked her lips, and watched his eyes darken and his lips drop even closer to hers.

Don't miss *Snowflakes and Silver Linings*, available December 2013–the third and final installment from the Gingerbread Girls!